DEMCO

ALSO BY ANNA MYERS

Tulsa Burning

Anna Myers

Walker & Company
New York

This book is dedicated with love to

JOHN CALVIN

who gave me Nobe and so much more

First published in the United States of America in 2002 by
Walker Publishing Company, Inc.

Published simultaneously in Canada by Fitzhenry and Whiteside,
Markham, Ontario L3R 4T8

For information about permission to reproduce sections from this book,
write to Permissions, Walker & Company, 435 Hudson Street,
New York, New York 10014

Library of Congress Cataloging-in-Publication Data
Myers, Anna.
  Tulsa burning / Anna Myers.
    p. cm.
  Summary: In 1921, fifteen-year-old Noble Chase hates the sheriff of
Wekiwa, Oklahoma, and is more than willing to cross him to help his best
friend, a black man, who is injured during race riots in nearby Tulsa.
  ISBN 0-8027-8829-7
  [1. Race relations—Fiction.   2. Coming of age—Fiction.   3. Interpersonal
relations—Fiction.   4. Fathers and sons—Fiction.   5. Riots—Fiction.
6. Oklahoma—History—20th century—Fiction.] I. Title.
PZ7.M9814 Tu 2002
[Fic]—dc21   2002023457

Visit Walker & Company at www.walkerbooks.com

Book design by Jennifer Daddio

Printed in the United States of America

2   4   6   8   10   9   7   5   3   1

Chapter I

I NEVER HAD ME but three friends. Last spring right after I turned fifteen, I lost one and almost lost the other two. I lost Rex, Isaac nearly died, and I near about lost Cinda because of impure thoughts. I never knew much about hating or about how wanting revenge eats away your insides until last spring. Truth be told, there's a bunch I didn't know until last spring. Sometimes I wish awful bad that I had never had to learn.

First off, I'll tell you about my name, Noble Wayne Chase. The first name is the same as my grandpa's on my ma's side. His name was Noble, and he had one brother named Worthy and one named Loyal. His sisters were named Patience and Joy. I can't tell you about the others, but I reckon my grandpa lived up to his name. He died when I was just a baby, but my ma used to tell me about him all the time. He was a black-smith, and he helped lots of people with stuff like building houses around the little town of Wekiwa, Oklahoma, back when it used to be an Indian village. I wish I could have knowed my grandpa named Noble.

Nobody except Mrs. Mitchell, Isaac's mother, has ever

called me anything but Nobe. Mrs. Mitchell is the teacher at the colored school down the road. She lives just about a half mile from us. After I got big enough to sell milk, Mrs. Mitchell always bought a jug from me every day, even after Isaac left home. "I've started drinking lots of milk myself," she told me, but I was pretty sure she just didn't want to cut down the money she gave me.

Pa would have throwed a ring-tailed fit if he'd ever known how I tagged after Isaac. Pa didn't like coloreds. He didn't like me selling milk to Mrs. Mitchell either, but he didn't try to make me quit because we needed every cent of money we could get our hands on. Ma always said she didn't have nothing against the Mitchells for being colored. She said God made colored folks same as he made whites.

I ain't sure Ma told the truth about not thinking coloreds was different, because she sure didn't like it that Mrs. Mitchell and Isaac lived in a nice solid little house with boxes of flowers on the windowsills. It was a lot better house than ours, and I noticed Ma's expression would sort of turn sour when we drove the wagon past the Mitchell place to go over and visit Widow Carter. She wouldn't admit it, but I'm pretty sure it bothered Ma, coloreds living better than we did.

I didn't care nothing about what color they was or about them having a better house. The important things to me was that Isaac always treated me good and that when Mrs. Mitchell talked to me, I felt like Noble, like I might grow up to do good things, things like my grandpa Noble used to do.

I reckon I'm on the scrawny side, which ain't surprising, considering how my stomach never was real full unless I ate down at the Mitchell place. My hair was yellow when I was just a young'un, but it has kind of got beyond that now to be almost brown. My eyes are blue, and they are weak, watering a bunch if I read a lot. My eyes are quick, though. They always told me when Pa got a mean spell on. My feet are quick too. I could outrun him to hide even when I was little. I had me a special place in the barn, one where me and Rex hid, one Pa never could find. When I got older, I figured out that me and Rex could just walk off for a spell. To Pa I was just something to hit if the hitting was easy, not something to go out of his way for.

I don't need to walk off or hide from Pa anymore. He died last spring, just after I turned fifteen and just before I learned about hate and revenge. I reckon everything really started the day he was buried. I remember standing beside Ma while Preacher Jackson read from the Bible. The preacher ain't none too strong, and he breathed sort of heavy as he read. Some of the neighbors stood around us. There was Cinda with her folks, Mr. and Mrs. Phillips. Widow Carter and her brother, who wasn't quite right in the head because of the war, were there. So was Mr. and Mrs. Collins and three of their kids. Sheriff Leonard was there with his puffed-up face and his red nose. Off a few steps from the others stood Mrs. Mitchell and Isaac.

I looked at Mrs. Mitchell, and her eyes were kind and gentle, like she was saying she understood. Mrs. Mitchell had seen the bruises Pa left on me. "Your father is not a good man, Noble," she told me once. "Don't let him decide your future for you." She handed me a saucer with a piece of hot apple pie and poured me a glass of milk from the jar she had just paid me for. "You are a bright young man, and you must stay in school."

Well, I thought, Pa won't be complaining about school

being a waste of time now. Pa wouldn't ever yell at me again. There would be no more bruises. I looked over at my mother's tired face. Ma's face was always tired, but never as tired as it was yesterday when she drove the wagon back from town.

It was on toward dark when I seen her coming, turning the wagon off the main road onto the long drive. I leaned against the barn, watching. Only Ma could be seen. Was Pa stretched out in the back, like when they left to see the doctor?

I waited for the wagon to move slowly down the drive and stop, finally, in front of the barn.

Ma got down from the wagon without looking back, and I knowed for sure then that my pa was not in the wagon. It was me that helped Pa into the wagon, him leaning hard. It had seemed strange to have Pa touch me like that, to need me to lean against.

"We'll see the doctor," Ma had said, and they were gone down the tree-lined drive. I watched until they were out on the main road. I turned back to the barn then. Pa would have a fit if he was to come back and find the chores not done.

But Pa had not come back. "He's dead," Ma had said after she climbed down from the wagon. "He was gone before I got to town. Doc said it was most likely his heart, like I figured when the pain started. Same thing killed his pa the year we married." Ma ran her hand across her eyes. "I reckon you're starved." She looked closely at me, like she hadn't seen me good at first. "I'll fix you a bite to eat."

I followed her into the kitchen. I wanted to question her. What would we do without Pa? Could we still farm the land? I wanted to tell Ma I was glad, glad the man who never did give me no kind word was gone. It wasn't that simple, though, on account of I wanted to tell her I was sorry too. I wanted to be sorry. My pa was dead. Shouldn't I be sorry? I didn't say nothing. Instead I went to the washstand, poured water from the big pitcher into the tin pan, rubbed the homemade lye soap across my hands, and washed.

It was Ma that said something. "We'll be leaving this place," she said.

I whirled to look at her. "Why? We can work the place! You know we done most of the work our ownselves, not Pa."

She sighed and looked away from me to study the potato she had been peeling. "It's the bank, Nobe. Our note's due, and Charlie Carson ain't likely to give us no extension without your pa. Banks don't put no stock in half-growed boys and worn-out women." She began to take long slices from the potato in her hand. "No, we got to leave."

My heart beat fast. Leave this place? I had never known no other home. I looked around the house, and I thought about the outside. Leave the pond with the willow tree? Leave Ma's grapevines growing beside the porch and the patch of sunflowers in the front pasture? Leave the barn where I milked old Buttercup and where I liked to rest, wedged among the bales up in the loft with the sweet hay smell like a salve for my hurts?

Ma had gone back to work, like I wasn't even there beside her, waiting. Finally I spoke. "Where? Where can we go?"

"Into Wekiwa, we'll have to go to town. Sheriff Leonard says they need help at their place, his wife being sickly and all. He says she don't get up most days a'tall, and she needs someone there to be with her."

I swallowed hard. I hated Sheriff Leonard, hated the way the man's bulging eyes looked at my mother when he brought Pa home drunk. Those awful eyes followed Ma around the room in a way that made me want to hit him, but of course I did not hit the man whose badge flashed even in the dim light from the lantern.

"Ma, not the sheriff's place!"

"It's a fine place, indoor toilet and all, three stories high. There's two rooms up on that top floor for you and me. Won't it be a wonder living in a house where the roof don't ever leak?"

"Please, Ma. We can think of something else." I shoved my knotted fists into the pocket of my worn-out overalls and searched for words. It wasn't likely I'd be able to come out and talk about what I knew Sheriff Leonard had in mind for Ma. She knew too, didn't she? I had to ask.

I drew in a breath and let go with the question. "Ma, you know the sheriff has got ideas about you. You know that, don't you?" I didn't look at her, just kept my eyes down.

"Son," she said, and her voice was weary. "I got no plans to do anything that ain't decent, but I got to think of the future. The sheriff's wife ain't likely to live much longer. There's money there, Nobe. If I was to marry Sheriff Leonard—" She paused for a minute, then went on. "Why, boy, there'd be ways to do things for you. Maybe you could go off to one of them colleges like that Mitchell boy did."

I stared at her. "Don't be making no such plans on my account," I said. "I don't want none of the sheriff's money, and I don't want to live in his fine house with you hoping his wife will pass on soon."

Anger flashed across her face. "I never done no planning before I married your pa." There was a break in her voice, and for a minute I thought she might cry, but she didn't. "Now he's laying in the back of Jones Furniture Store, stone cold and waiting for Roscoe Jones to make him a box." She pointed to the skillet. "See them taters. They're nearabout the last food we got." She shook her head. "Oh, we could find a neighbor to take us in, be someone's charity. No, I got to plan for the future." There was no trace of a sob in her voice toward the end, only flatness and a terrible final sound.

"I'm going out," I said. "I'll be back when supper's ready."

"You done washed," she protested, but I went anyway, through the back screen door onto the porch. The spring night met me with the cry of what seemed like a thousand tree frogs, and I breathed in deep gulps of the soft air, trying to forget everything but the night and its sounds.

Old Rex came to me, and I dropped down on the edge of the porch to stroke the dog's back. "Good old boy," I said, "we're leaving this place. Ma's planning for our future." A moan come up from inside me then, a moan born from a sudden and certain thought. "He won't want a dog," I whispered, and I pressed my face against the top of the dog's head, "but I won't go without you. I won't take a step toward that sheriff's fine house, not without you, boy!"

Ma called me then, and I went inside. Dinner was on the table. I slid onto the bench, bent over my plate, and went to filling my mouth with fried potatoes and onions. Ma brought her own plate to come and settle across from me, but she only took a bite or two. We didn't do no talking. When I was done eating, I carried my plate to the rickety cook table and set it next to the dishpan. Then I went back outside.

Rex stayed beside me. For a real long time we walked through the fields and pasture. If I kicked a rock, I'd start to bend over and pick it up, but I stopped myself. I wouldn't be trying to plow these fields no more. I was done with fighting the rocks. I figured the rocks could have the place now. When I got too tired to make my feet move good, we went back to the house and settled on the ground beneath the big cottonwood near the barn. From there I could see my ma's bedroom window. Soon a lantern light appeared there briefly before she blew it out.

"She's in bed now, so I can go inside," I said to Rex. I went into the house, blew out the lantern on the kitchen table, made my way to the tiny room at the side of the house, and threw myself on the narrow bed.

THAT'S WHAT HAPPENED before we buried Pa. The next day, standing beside the grave, I could feel Sheriff Leonard looking at me. I tried not to think about the stinking sheriff, just kept my eyes on the preacher, who was talking about heaven. It was purely impossible for me to believe Preacher Jackson had any real hope that Melvin Chase could make it to heaven. Everyone around our place and in the small town of Wekiwa knowed that my pa was a drunk. It didn't seem likely to me that God would let a man who had once puked right on the church steps during Sunday service into heaven. Pa had never done one thing good that I knowed of.

Suddenly I closed my eyes, remembering. There was that one time. I was four, so that made it eleven years ago. It was summer, and I had gone out into the backyard with no shoes. I went to pick little purple wildflowers for my ma, and I got right in a big patch of stickers. At first I just hollered out, but then I realized no one was coming to help me. Standing on one foot, I picked up the other one, turned it up, and started to remove the stickers, but I lost my balance and tumbled into the thorny patch. My legs, protected by overalls, were fine, but I didn't have on no shirt. Now my back was full of stickers too. I just gave up, closed my eyes, and sobbed.

Then I felt myself being lifted, higher than I ever had been lifted before. The arms were strong, and I knowed, even without opening my eyes, that it was my pa who lifted me. "He'll hurt me now," I thought. My pa always hit me if I cried, and forgetting the stickers in my back, I drew myself as much as possible into a ball and waited for the blow.

"Don't cry, little man," a voice said. I thought the voice was my pa's voice, but I couldn't never remember Pa ever talking soft like to me before. "Let's get those burrs out of you, and you'll quit the hurting."

The man's face was close to mine. This could not be my pa; there wasn't no smell like the one that came from Pa's bottles and stayed on his breath. Afraid, I opened just one eye to peek. It *was* my pa! He carried me into the house and put me on the kitchen bench. Pa took out every sticker. With his own hands, he done that. Next he wet a cloth with water warm from the tea kettle and washed my face, back, and feet. Then, without a word, he kissed the top of my head and went out the back door.

Now, remembering, I touched the top of my own head. Oh, Pa, I thought, why couldn't you ever be that way again? I remembered trying once, a few weeks later, to re-create the scene by going on purpose into the stickers when my pa was nearby.

I yelled out in pain, but my pa, cursing, just left me there and disappeared into the barn. I stayed in that sticker patch, crying, for a long time. Ain't no use of bawling, I finally told myself. You might as well give it up. I bit my lip and crawled out of them stickers. One place on my hand had blood on it, but I didn't do no more crying. I couldn't remember much crying at all after that day, but now, standing beside my pa's grave, I felt one tear slip from my eye and roll down my cheek.

Chapter 2

WHEN THE PREACHER STOPPED TALKING, I realized it was time to cover the box. Preacher Jackson took a shovel, stuck it into the earth, and tossed the dirt onto the box. Lucky it's springtime when we get lots of rain, I thought. The preacher didn't look strong enough to dig in Oklahoma earth when it was dry. He filled the shovel again and handed it to Ma.

When Ma had tossed her dirt on the box, the preacher took the shovel back. He started to put it in the ground again, but I stepped over and took it from him. I could fill my own shovel with dirt to throw on Pa's grave.

When it was over, I stood looking at the mound of dirt and thinking that Pa was really gone. Used to be that he controlled our lives even when he was gone from home. This time would be different. There wouldn't be no homecoming when he'd cuss or throw the coffeepot full of hot coffee. I expected to get some feeling of lightness knowing it was over with him, but there wasn't no relief in the knowledge, only a strange aching emptiness. I looked at the grave and wished I could buy him some kind of headstone.

Ma and me were the first to move. We left the neighbor men with their hats in their hands and the women with sad eyes. Cinda Phillips took after us and pulled at my arm. "Heard you'all are moving to town," she said softly.

"Reckon that's so," I managed to say, but I couldn't look at Cinda. Lately, I'd started to be uncomfortable around her on account of the impure thoughts. See, me and Cinda have been friends since we was six years old, but just a few months ago I noticed that Cinda didn't look the same. Her chest wasn't flat no more. I reckon that's normal and all.

It's me that ain't normal or decent. I spend a lot of time fighting them impure thoughts, but it ain't easy. I try just to think about how we got to be friends. She had just moved into the house down the road from our place, and I walked by there on my way to school. She was standing beside her swing under the mulberry tree in the front yard.

"We could walk to school together," she yelled, and she smiled her big smile that showed both front teeth were missing.

I felt real bashful, just looked down at my bare feet and didn't say nothing. I'd seen Cinda out in front of her place when we drove by in the wagon, and once she come with her mother to sit on the front porch with Ma. "Her name's Cinda," Ma told me, but I just ducked behind my ma's skirt.

"What's wrong with you, little boy?" Cinda asked me on that first school morning. "Has the cat got your tongue?"

"I'm not a little boy," I told her. "I'm big as you. Maybe bigger." I moved over to stand beside Cinda, measuring with my eyes how her red pig-tailed head measured against my blond one.

We didn't say nothing to each other, just started walking

the half mile to the school. Just outside the one-room school-house, I stopped, suddenly just too scared to go inside. I stepped back away from the door. "I can't go to school," I said. "I don't know nothing about reading or numbers."

Cinda reached out to grab my hand. "Come on, silly," she said. "You ain't supposed to know nothing when you first go to school. We're going to have us a teacher and books."

For eight years we walked to school together. Last year we finished at the little school down the road. Pa didn't see no sense in me going to town for high school, but Cinda's pa drove us into Wekiwa, us hunkered down in the back of his old truck. Up front was one seat just big enough for the driver. The rest of the cab was filled with glass jugs of milk that Mr. Phillips would deliver to customers in town. Sometimes Mr. Phillips picked us up after school. Sometimes we walked the three miles home. If Pa was out on a drunk, Ma might drive the wagon into town to get us.

It made me mad at myself for having them impure thoughts that made me so uncomfortable with Cinda. When she caught up with me and Ma at the cemetery, I just looked down at my shoes while she talked. "It'll be sort of lonesome for me on the ride to school next year," she said.

I opened up my mouth to say something to her, but no words come to my mind. I just stood there, too dadgum dumb to talk. Ma saved me. "We'll be living over at Sheriff and Mrs. Leonard's place," she said, and she put her hand on Cinda's shoulder. "You come by there and say hey, to us, you hear?"

Ma moved off a little, and Cinda turned back to me. "I want you to take this," she said, and she took something out of her dress pocket. She reached over, took my hand, and dropped a cold, hard object into it. I opened my fingers and looked down at her lucky silver dollar.

"No." I shook my head. "I can't take this. You use it to win races and stuff."

She laughed. "Haven't you noticed we don't run races at high school? You need luck right now more than I do, living with the sheriff and all."

"You use it for other stuff too, like the test."

Just last year me and Cinda went over to the county seat to the courthouse and took the county exam that eighth-graders take if they want to go on to high school. Cinda took out her lucky silver dollar, and she laid it between our desks, real careful to make it exactly between us. "This way it will bring us both luck," she said.

After a while, my eyes went to feeling tired and started watering. I was rubbing at them when Cinda looked over at me. She looked worried, like my eyes might keep me from passing the test. Then she stuck out her leg and used her foot to scoot the silver dollar as close to my desk as she could get it. I reckon it worked. I made a real high score on that test. Cinda did all right too. The way I figure it is that Cinda is the kind that will do all right, always.

Now she was wanting to give me her most valuable possession. "I wouldn't feel right," I said, and I held it out to her.

She put her hands behind her back. "Please. You can give it back to me later, but I want you to have it now."

"Well, okay," I said. "I suspect I will be needing luck."

Just then her pa called out for her to come along, and she hurried off. I headed to the wagon. I knew folks were passing by me, but I didn't feel none like talking. I leaned my head down against the wood side of the wagon. Out of the corner of my eye I saw Widow Carter and her brother stop a few feet away. "We're real sorry, boy," she said. I nodded. The widow's brother, Olly, was sometimes too addled to know what went on around him. But sometimes he had real clear spells, like today. Olly left his sister's side to come and touch my shoulder.

It pleased me to have Olly wanting to comfort me on account of him being an expert on hurting. I raised my head and looked into his eyes, brown and knowing.

Widow Carter come over to lead her brother away, and I realized Mrs. Mitchell and Isaac was standing on my other side.

Isaac didn't say nothing, just reached out and punched me on the shoulder. It was our way, what we did when we first seen each other after Isaac come home from college or how we'd say good-bye when he was fixing to go back. Isaac was done with college now, and he worked over in Tulsa. I knowed he was missing a day's work to come to see my pa get buried just so he could punch me on the shoulder.

"I'll miss our talks," Mrs. Mitchell said.

"Mr. Phillips is going to bring you good milk, though," I said. Then my misery come busting out. "I don't want to live in that man's house," I said.

"But you will. Your mother needs you."

I couldn't say nothing about my ma. I was too ashamed knowing she was planning to be real handy when the sheriff took to looking for a second wife.

Mrs. Mitchell looked over her shoulder to make sure no one was around before she talked more. Then she said, "Be careful. Sheriff Leonard has bad things inside him, and they sometimes come spewing out. Just remember your name. You may need more than ever to be truly Noble." Then she walked away, her dark head held high.

Ma was moving toward me by then, and Sheriff Leonard walked close behind her. "Let me help you, Vivian," he said when Ma started to climb up to the wagon seat.

"I'll help her," I said quick, and I took her arm.

Sheriff Leonard put his big straw hat back on his head, spit his tobacco to the side, and gave me a long look. "Might as well take that chip off your shoulder, son," he drawled. "We're likely to be seeing lots of one another in days to come. Don't it seem like we ought to get to be friends?"

"Never had me many friends," I said.

"Suit yourself, then, son." He looked up at Ma. "I'll follow you, Vivian. The missus is real anxious to get you settled in."

He moved on to the big black car marked "Sheriff."

I got Ma settled, climbed onto the driver's seat, and told the horses, "Get up." I waited for Ma to scold me on account of me acting like I did toward the sheriff, but she stayed totally silent, staring straight ahead. The cemetery is just at the edge of Wekiwa, so we had to drive three miles to home. When we turned up the driveway to our place, we seen the sheriff's car parked in front of the house.

Sheriff Leonard was in the front porch rocker. He got up and stretched as me and Ma walked toward him. "Take the horses to the barn, boy," he said. "Charlie Carson aims to send someone from the bank to get them and the cow and I reckon anything else on the place that can be sold. You'uns gather up your clothes and whatnot. I'll just set here and rest a spell."

I did what he said, unhitched the horses from the wagon, and put them in the stall. "Well, old boys," I said, "I guess I won't be seeing you after this." I threw in some extra hay. Next I moved to the cow and patted her rump. What would I do in town with no farm chores to tend to? Once I would have loved the idea of leaving all that work behind. Now I hated it.

I went through the back door into the dark kitchen. My mother moved around the house, dropping things into a big basket. I watched her take the family Bible from a table in the parlor. Then I couldn't watch anymore, and I went into my room.

It didn't take long to get my clothes, two pair of overalls, two shirts, an extra pair of summer underwear, and my winter longhandles. No use to take my beat-up winter coat. I should have thrown it in the fire last winter. It was too little and too worn out then to do me any real good. I wouldn't even be able to squeeze into it by the time cold weather came again. There wasn't much else to gather up. I got my knife, the jar of marbles I'd won after Isaac taught me to play real good, and the lucky horseshoe my grandpa had made for me with my name, Noble, forged right into it. The last thing I did was to take the keys from the very back of my shelf where I hid them.

I held the keys in my hand and stared down at their thin black shape. I'd made one of them keys myself after a bunch of studying. The thing is, I've always been interested in metal work, made me a knife using a file on a strip of steel when I wasn't more than eight or nine.

Hanging around the blacksmith shop in town was just about my favorite thing to do. Old Elmer Keller got so he'd let me use his hammers and tools anytime he wasn't working on a big job. Horseshoes were Elmer's main work, and since so many folks had got themselves automobiles, Elmer didn't have as much work as he used to have.

Well, last winter, I used Elmer's shop to make one of these

black keys, and I had used the keys to keep me and Ma from starving to death. Now I was looking down at them, wondering if I'd ever have the nerve to use them black keys while I was sleeping at the sheriff's house. I shook my head. No, likely I wouldn't, but I might use them to get away from the sheriff's house. I dropped the keys down in the pocket of my good black pants. If I had to use them, it wouldn't be the first time I had to steal from the telephone company.

The first time it happened was last winter. It was late one night when I walked down the main street of Wekiwa looking for Pa because he'd been gone five days. He hadn't been drunk when he left, said he thought he could pick up a day or so of work in town, cleaning up for some storekeeper. He hadn't come home.

Finally, I set off to look for him. I pulled at the collar of that worn-out coat, trying to get it up around my freezing ears. The sleeves was too short, and my arms turned red with cold. Supper hadn't been nothing but thin hard biscuits, made without no baking powder or soda, the same biscuits we'd been living on for almost a week.

Usually we had stuff Ma had put away from the garden, but last summer's drought pretty much done the garden in. Ma's canned goods had only lasted through December.

Now it was February, and I was sure hungry. I stopped in front of the town's only eating place, Daisy's Café. Pa wouldn't be inside there, but I decided to step in, just long enough to breathe some warm air. The smell of beef stew filled the place, and I could see a big bowl in front of a man at the first table. My knees went to feeling weak, and I sort of leaned against the door.

The owner, Daisy Harrison, come toward me. "Do you want to order something?" she asked.

I shook my head. "No money." I mouthed the words, too ashamed to say them out loud.

"You come with me," Daisy said, and I steadied myself, then followed her through the swinging doors into the kitchen. She pointed at a small table with a chair. "Set yourself down," she said, and she dipped up a bowl of stew for me.

I reckon no food ever tasted so good to me, but I hated to be given a handout. When I left, I muttered a quick "thanks," without even looking at Daisy Harrison.

I got out of the door quick and moved down the street, cussing my pa. I didn't stop until I was in front of the drugstore, which was closed. Trying to figure what to do next, I leaned on the building, my shoulder against the pay phone. It wasn't long till a man I didn't know stopped his automobile and come toward me. "Would you mind moving, so's I can make a call?" the stranger asked me.

I took a few steps, but I watched as the man dropped coins into the slot. He tried to make a call then, but he ended up pounding on the phone. "Dang thing stole my money," he yelled to nobody in particular. "Reckon it's busted."

I never had really put no thought into how a telephone like that worked. I started to wonder where the money went. I could see the box. The money couldn't go through them little telephone lines. No, the money had to still be in that box. When the stranger put up that receiver, I went back to that telephone box, and I studied the keyholes.

I never could have been a telephone thief if what happened next had not happened. Lo and behold, a man in a telephone truck drove up just then. I moved on down the street a little so he wouldn't notice me, but I leaned against a door watching him. He took the money out of that pay telephone. Then he took it off the wall, put it on his truck, got a new one, and put it on.

When the man went into the café to eat, I took the phone off his truck, and I run with it. I was scared to death, and I kept looking back over my shoulder. The phone was pretty heavy, and I knowed I couldn't run far. I headed for some trees that grow around a little creek just back of Main Street. There I dropped down on the brown grass and went to studying that phone.

It had two locks on it, one back on the side and one in the front. The amazing thing was that in the side lock I found a key, a little strip of metal with sort of waves in it. I turned my attention to the front lock, and I got a good idea. In my pocket, I had a piece of gum. Cinda had give it to me the day before at school, and I was saving it for when hunger got too much, and I just had to have some taste besides my own spit in my mouth.

I took out the stick of gum, just wet it a little in my mouth, and eased it into the lock. Ever so careful, I pulled the gum out of the lock, and I had a great impression of the key. I'd take that key to the blacksmith's shop in town and ask to use his tools to make me a real key.

Then I started to worry about the phone man. When he missed the phone, what if he remembered me watching him? He could ask around town and learn my name. Besides, he might figure out what I was doing. He might even take away Wekiwa's one pay phone.

The man might still be in the café. I had to see if I could return that phone, minus the key. Maybe he would think the key fell out, or maybe he had even forgot that he left it in. Even though it was freezing cold, I took off my worn-out coat and wrapped it around the phone. I knowed if the phone man saw me with the bundle, he'd figure right off what it was. The coat, though, would keep other folks from knowing.

First, I stored my gum key on a rock. Then I run back into town. When I got to the street where the truck was parked, I leaned around the corner of a building to look. The truck was still there. I didn't run, just walked along, natural, with my bundle under my arm.

I only passed one woman on the sidewalk. She didn't pay me no mind, just hurried by with her head down. No one else seemed to be around. I moved toward the truck. I had just re-placed the phone when someone yelled, "Hey!"

I jumped. The telephone man was coming off the side-walk toward me. "What are you doing, kid?" he demanded.

Had he seen me with the phone? My heart was pounding, and I thought maybe my mouth was too dry to talk, but I got something out. "I was just looking at this here truck," I said. "Are you the fellow that gets to drive it? That sure must be a grand job." I reached out and sort of stroked the truck, amazed at what a good liar I could be.

He laughed. "I am," he said, "but it ain't as much fun as you make it sound." He got in then and drove away, leaving me there too weak to move on.

Five times last winter I used them keys. I figured it wouldn't be smart to take all the money. The phone company man was bound to get suspicious if there wasn't no money a'tall in the box when he come to collect. Besides, I was al-ways hoping I wouldn't need to use the keys to keep me and Ma from starving again.

"Where'd you get the money for all this?" Ma asked me when I brought the groceries home that first time.

I let on like I didn't hear her, just kept setting food from the box onto the table. I had hitched the horses to the wagon, and without telling Ma where, I drove into town to buy the meat, potatoes, cans of corn, peas, carrots, and green beans. "I was thinking maybe you could make some stew," I said. "Stew tastes real good when it's cold as blazes outside."

Ma took the package of meat and stroked the white paper covering it. Then she untied the string, took off the paper, and held the meat up in front of her to admire. "Stew sure does sound good," she said, and she moved to take down the big kettle that hung over the wood stove. But she stopped still, holding the kettle above her head. "Son, I want to know how you come up with the money for these goods!"

I just shrugged. "What difference does it make how I done it. It's done, and I don't see as how I got to talk about it." Ma's face looked all hurt and fearful, and I softened. "Well," I said, "don't make me talk about it now, Ma. I'll tell you sometime."

It wasn't no easy thing, facing Ma after I had stolen money, but it was even harder going to Mrs. Mitchell's place. I had to take her milk, though. I waited till after I had my stomach full of Ma's stew. The wind had died down, but it was still plenty cold. I didn't hitch up the horses, though. Somehow, I thought that it was right, me walking in the cold. I reckon I was hoping somehow that it would make me feel better, sort of like I was paying for the stealing by being cold.

I tried whistling to sort of keep my mind off things, but when I got close to Mrs. Mitchell's house, I couldn't keep the whistling up. I took to hoping she wouldn't be home. If she was gone, I could go inside and leave the milk. She could pay me the twenty cents later. She was there, though. I could see a lantern's light, and the automobile Isaac had bought her a few months before was parked near the door.

"I'm coming," she called as soon as I knocked. "Oh, Noble," she said when she opened the door, "come right in out of the cold. You are such a good boy, bringing my milk through the cold night. You could have waited until tomorrow."

I'd been feeling pretty low already, but her saying I was good made me just plumb miserable. I stepped inside and set the milk jar on the kitchen table. "No, ma'am," I said. "I sure enough am not good, and I ain't Noble either, and you shouldn't call me that." I stepped back toward the door.

"Noble is your name, and Noble you are," she said, and she peered at my face real close like. "I know a thing or two about boys, the good ones and the ones too troubled to be good. I raised one of the good ones myself." She waved her hand in the direction of the fireplace mantel and the big picture of Isaac. "I've taught a great many boys, many of them good and some of the troubled ones too. Boys are the same, white or colored. I know a good boy when I see one, and you, Noble Chase, are undoubtedly one of the good ones. What, I am wondering, would make you think otherwise?"

"It's nothing, I reckon," I said. "But it ain't easy deciding what's good and what ain't." I shrugged. "The world ain't a very good place as I see it, awful cold and hungry."

"Are you hungry, child? Gracious! I should have asked already. I have a big piece of ham left over from my supper, and I baked bread yesterday." She moved toward her small icebox.

"No." I took another backward step toward the door. "I ain't hungry a'tall. I just had me two big bowls of stew."

"You're sure?"

I nodded my head, turned, and reached for the door handle. "I'm awful sorry, Mrs. Mitchell," I muttered.

"For what?"

For a second I couldn't answer. I couldn't tell her what I done. Then I thought of something to say. "I keep forgetting and saying 'ain't,' and you asked me not to use the word. I'm awful sorry."

She smiled at me. "It's all right. I've no doubt that you will learn, Noble. I've no doubt that you will grow up to be well educated."

"I don't know, but thank you, ma'am." I stepped out into the night.

"You will be good too," Mrs. Mitchell added. "Just as you are right now."

I didn't have nothing to say, just let on like I didn't hear her and headed off into the cold night. When last winter was over, I told myself I wouldn't never use them black keys again, but I didn't throw them away, just stuck them way back on my shelf. Finally, in the spring Pa sold a calf, and Ma got the money hid away before he could drink it up. Now I was putting them keys in my pocket, thinking I might use them if I had to escape from Sheriff Leonard's place.

"Come along, son," Ma called from the next room. "Dudley will be getting impatient."

Dudley! So Ma had taken to using the sheriff's first name. What would be next? The idea made me sick, but the name made me smile. Dudley! I hadn't never heard his given name before. Dudley! That was awful close to Dud. That's what I'd call him in my mind and under my breath. Sheriff Leonard was a Dud of a man, well known for bullying poor people, especially the colored folks. No wonder Mrs. Mitchell warned me to be careful.

I rolled my clothes into a bundle with my marble jar and horseshoe in the middle of it. Then I looked around one last time at the little room I'd always slept in. Ma waited near the front door. "Hurry," she said. "We can't be taking advantage of the sheriff's kindness."

"We sure enough cannot, because there ain't no such thing as that man's kindness." I moved toward the door. "He'll expect to be repaid, Ma, and you know it as sure as I do."

That made her as mad as a wet hen, and she whirled to look back at me. "Nobe," she said, but she got interrupted by a shout from outside.

"Vivian, will you get that kid of yours out here! We got to get a move on. I ain't got all day to fritter away. I got law work to see to."

Ma scurried for the door. "We're coming, Dudley, right this very minute."

Sheriff Leonard had left the front-porch rocking chair. He set behind the steering wheel of his automobile, his door still open. The minute I set foot on the porch, Rex come running to me. I bent to stroke the dog's back. "Come on, boy," I said, "we've got to go for a ride."

"Don't be thinking you'uns is bringing that mangy critter," the sheriff called.

I froze there beside my dog. "Please, Ma," I begged, "I can't leave Rex."

She looked at me, then back out toward the sheriff. She sighed. "Dudley," she called, "the dog means a powerful lot to the boy."

The sheriff heaved his great bulk real quick like from

the automobile. "You heard me, woman. I said the dog ain't going!"

"Then don't be waiting for me." I got up, stepped off the porch, and headed toward the barn. Rex trotted beside me.

"Suit your own self then," shouted the sheriff. "I wasn't crazy about having no scruffy kid like you around anyways, but don't be thinking as you'll hang around this house. Charlie Carson's likely done got plans to put his brother-in-law on the place."

"Nobe, honey," Ma called, "be reasonable." I looked back to see her twisting her hands together. "The new folks will likely feed Rex," she said, "and you know yourself that dog will be happier right here than in town."

Ignoring them both, I just kept walking. "Dudley, please," Ma said, "I can't leave the boy out here all alone with nothing."

I didn't turn and look, so I never saw the sheriff take his gun from the holster he wore. I did hear my ma scream, but by then the bullet had found its target. Rex fell down to the ground. For a second, I was too addled to realize what had happened. Then I moaned and dropped down beside my dog.

"Rex," I pleaded, "don't be dead. You can't be dead, boy." Rex did not move. His eyes stared straight ahead. I put my hand on Rex's side and felt no breath coming out of him. I could feel hot tears gathering up behind my eyes, but I fought them back. I would not cry! I just wouldn't! I hated them both, my ma just the same as the sheriff. I wouldn't never let either of them see me cry!

Ma pulled on my arm. "I'm sorry, son, so sorry, but we're obliged to go."

"I'm going to bury him, Ma. You can go on with the sheriff if you want to, or maybe 'Dudley' will just decide to shoot me too. Don't matter. I'm not leaving until I bury my dog." Without ever looking at her, I got up, went to the barn, and come back with a shovel.

"Please, Dudley. The boy's been hurt a great lot." Ma's words carried to my ears as I carried Rex and the shovel toward the cottonwood tree. I hated the syrupy sweet tone in her voice, pleading with the man who just got done shooting my dog.

Don't think about the sheriff now, I told myself. Hate was a bitter taste in my mouth, but I knowed I couldn't fight the man and his badge. There wouldn't be no way of beating him. Not now, but the day would come. It had to! That was the minute I started living for revenge! I put all my energy into digging the hole. When the grave was dug and Rex was covered, I went to the big black automobile. Ma and "Dudley" had been standing under the shade of an oak tree. They come and got into the car. It didn't surprise me none that Ma got up front with him.

I crawled into the backseat. I didn't speak a word to either of them, and I didn't look back either. As the big automobile pulled away from the only home I had ever knowed, I just kept my eyes on one thing, the clenched fists I held in my lap.

Chapter 3

THE THREE-MILE RIDE into the town of Wekiwa did not take long. Sheriff Leonard drove fast, and even with the windows down, the smell of his cigar made me feel even sicker than I already was. Everything about the man made me sick, and I figured I'd better work at blocking out the conversation between him and my ma, else I might puke right there in his sheriff's automobile. I just kept repeating to myself, I'll get revenge. Someday I'll make Mr. Dudley Leonard sorry he ever heard of Nobe Chase.

We stopped in front of a large white house. I thought about how I'd seen the place a hundred times, but since I never had any notion I'd end up living there, I had never paid it any real mind. Things sure had changed. Now I leaned toward the side window, wanting to get a good look. There was big shade trees in the front yard and a swing on the big front porch. The house was trimmed in yellow and had yellow shutters at the windows. There was a white picket fence around the place.

"It's beautiful," Ma said from the front seat. I thought so too. It didn't seem right, a man like the sheriff living in such a beautiful place. He come around to open the door for Ma and to take the box of things she held on her lap.

"Come on inside," he said. "Mavis will be anxious to meet you two."

I got out and followed with my bundle under my arm. I still kept my fists clenched tight. The screen door opened into a wide hall with shiny wood floors. The entire place smelled good. Then I seen why. A table stood beside the stairs, and on the table was a vase with white roses in it.

"Mavis is up in her room," the sheriff explained. "She don't never come down unless I carry her. I'll take you there first. Then you can take your things on up to the third-floor bedrooms." I was following behind, and he turned back to me. "My wife ain't strong," he said. "She's not never to be troubled! Do you understand me? She'll be asking how you feel about living here, and you're fixing to tell her you're pleased as punch." He leaned back down the stairs to be close to me, and I could feel his hot breath on my face. "I've got me a leather whip my papa used to use on slaves back in Mississippi! It ain't been used much lately, but I been thinking of getting it out and practicing." He grabbed at my shirt. "You understanding me, boy?"

I wanted to spit at him, but instead I nodded my head yes.

"Speak up," he said, low and mean. "Don't be shaking your fool head at me. Say 'yes, sir' when I ask you a question."

"Yes, sir," I said, and I swallowed back the vomit that come up into my throat.

In the upstairs hall I seen an open door. "Is that you, Dudley?" a voice called from the room. "I'm so glad you are here!"

"It's me, darlin'," the sheriff called. "I've brung Mrs. Chase and her son with me. They're just busting to meet you."

"Wonderful," said the voice. "Bring them to me, please."

I followed Ma and Sheriff Leonard into the room. In the middle of the room was a great big bed with four high posts. Spread out up high over the posts was a kind of lacy cover. For a minute I was so taken with looking that bed over that I forgot to look at the woman in it.

Then I noticed her there in the middle of the bed, propped up against some big pillows. No wonder the sheriff could carry her downstairs. I never saw such a big bed or such a tiny woman. She held a hand mirror in front of her face. "Mercy," she said, "my hair's a fright today." She pushed at wisps of faded red hair until they went behind her ear. Then she put down the mirror and gave a nervous little laugh. "But that's no way to greet folks, is it?" She held her hand out to Ma.

"How'd you do," Ma said. She took the hand and bowed over it slightly. "I'm Vivian Chase, and this here's my boy, Nobe." Ma reached back to pull me closer to the bed. "Say hello, son."

"Hello," I said. The tiny woman smiled at me. There was something real warm and sweet about her smile. She smelled good too, and I could see a can of talcum powder on the table by the bed. If I could have, I would of smiled back at Mrs. Leonard, but I just didn't have no smiles inside me. I could feel her studying my face, real interested in what she saw there.

"Mercy, you remind me of my younger brother." She leaned closer to me. "He was lots younger than me, just a baby when I left home, but my, how I loved him." She turned toward the sheriff. "You see the likeness, don't you, Dudley? This boy's so much like Joe."

"Don't know as I do," said the sheriff.

Mrs. Leonard waved her hand toward a framed picture on the wall. "That's Joe," she said.

The young man had on a soldier's suit, and his nose and eyes reminded me of myself, except that he had a real happy look on his face, lots happier than I figured I had ever looked.

"We lost Joe in the war. He died in France," she said softly. "Broke our hearts, didn't it, Dudley?"

I glanced real quick at the sheriff. His lip turned down for just a second, and a flicker come to his eyes that looked even meaner than usual. He sort of shook his head fast, and he got a fake sad look on his face. "Sure did, sugar. Broke our hearts."

I could see two things right then. Sheriff Dudley did not like his wife's younger brother, probably felt glad when he died. I could see too that the sheriff's wife was the boss in this house. I decided right then that it would be fun to watch that man hop when she said jump.

"Your brother was a fine-looking young man," my mother said. "That picture does put a body in mind of Nobe." She shook her head. "It's a terrible shame he had to die that way."

Mrs. Leonard smiled at Ma, then went back to looking at me, but she spoke to her husband. "Just look at this boy, Dudley," she said. "Surely you can see how like Joe he is."

The sheriff sort of shifted from one foot to the other. "Well, now that I look close, I reckon you're right."

Mrs. Leonard turned back to me. "Joe was always smiling, though, and you're a sad young thing," she said, and she shook her head. "Of course you are, burying your father just today." She patted my hand. "Well, we will just have to work at making you happy again, won't we, Dudley?" She turned to her husband who came to kiss her cheek.

"That we will," the sheriff said, just the same as if he meant it. The easy way he lied didn't surprise me none, but it made a cold shiver crawl up my spine.

My eyes traveled over to the sides of the bed. There was a case full of books, and books stacked on the floor too. One book laid facedown and open on Mrs. Leonard's lap. I could see it said *Huckleberry Finn* on the cover.

I reckon Mrs. Leonard saw me looking at the books. "They fill my days," she said, holding up the book. "Do you like to read, Nobe?"

"Can't very much," I said.

Ma spoke up right quick. "He don't mean he can't read, just that his eyes are weak, won't hold up to much reading." She patted my shoulder. "Nobe's a smart boy, done real well on the county exam, he did."

"Maybe he needs glasses." Mrs. Leonard leaned toward me and studied my face like she might figure out my eye problem by looking close. "We'll have to see what can be done about your eyes, Nobe."

"Do you reckon we ought to let these folks get settled in their rooms now, darlin'?" the sheriff asked.

"Oh, my mercy, yes," she said, "but Vivian"—She stopped and put her hand over her mouth. "Oh, dear, I forgot to ask if I may use your given name? Forgive me for being so bold."

Ma stepped up closer to the bed. "Why, sure, you can call me Vivian," she said.

"And you must call me Mavis." She clasped her hands together and put them against her thin face. "Oh, we are going to be so happy in this house now."

Another shiver traveled up my spine. I figured I might as

well get used to them shivers. This was a place bound to produce them.

"You'uns follow me," said the sheriff. Me and Ma trotted after him out of the room and up another flight of stairs. "That one's yours, boy," he told me when we was at the top. "You'll be expected to work around here to pay for your keep, but Mavis doesn't want you to start until tomorrow. Says you ought to have the rest of the day off."

I ducked into the small room, closed the door, and leaned against it, glad to shut out the sound of the conversation between Ma and the sheriff. I stared at the bare white walls, the cot, and the small corner table.

I took my marble jar and horseshoe out of my bundle and put them on the table. There was a shelf in the corner, so I put my roll of clothes there. I kept the silver dollar in my pocket. It hadn't brought me no good luck so far, but I wanted to keep it close to me, to remind me of Cinda.

Windows made up the walls on two sides of the room. I pushed back the curtains and looked down at the street below. A big lump come up in my throat. I was used to looking out at a barn and a pasture with sunflowers in it. Here I couldn't see nothing but town, almost the whole town of Wekiwa, Oklahoma. Right across from me was the post office, the jail, and Daisy's Café. I went to the last window in the row, and I could see the sidewalk for Hill's Grocery and Dry Goods Store just right of the sheriff's house. On the other side of Hill's was the blacksmith shop and the drugstore. Except for the Last Chance Baptist Church and the Wekiwa School, both off to the left of the sheriff's house, that was all there was to the town.

I stayed there at the window for a while. Down the street

I saw a boy I recognized from school. He come out of the grocery store, and he carried a box piled high with groceries. He put the box in a wagon parked in front of the sidewalk. Then he went back for another box. I watched him carry out three boxes. All the time my mind was working.

Maybe living in town wouldn't be all bad. I started wondering if the chores Sheriff Leonard had in mind for me would take all day. It didn't seem likely there would be that much work around the place. There ought to be time for me to work somewhere else too. If I was to ask the sheriff, though, he'd most likely say no to the idea of me getting a job just to spite me.

I opened my door and listened. No talking come from Ma's room. I wondered if she had gone back downstairs to Mrs. Leonard's room. Maybe I should go down there and talk to the sheriff's wife about getting a job. It was good, knowing that the sheriff did pretty much whatever his missus wanted done.

The bedroom door was open. I could hear Ma's voice even before I got to the door. She was talking about me. "Oh, yes, he's a good boy, never gave us a minute's trouble." Her words took on a sad sound. "His pa was awful hard on him, though. You might of heard that Melvin was turned to the bottle." It was quiet then, and I knowed that Mrs. Leonard was talking in her soft way.

I stepped up and knocked on the door frame. "Could I come in, please?" I asked.

Mrs. Leonard's weary face broke into a smile. "Oh, my, yes, you just come right in this room. My mercy, it makes me feel better already, just having a young one in the house. Oh, yes, it surely does."

I went in to stand beside the chair Ma had pulled up beside the bed. "Mrs. Leonard," I said, "I've got me a question, but maybe you'd rather I was to wait on your husband to answer it for me."

She smiled again. "Well, my gracious, you just ask me whatever you want to ask, and we'll just see do I know how to answer."

"Well, the sheriff, he mentioned that there'd be chores around your place here for me to do, to pay for my keep and such. Of course, that seems fair and all, but I was wondering, do you reckon how I'll be busy here all the time, or do you think maybe there'd be time for me to do work for someone else in town was I able to find someone to hire me?"

Mrs. Leonard leaned over to pat Ma's arm. "What a fine boy you've got there, Vivian. Wanting to work straight off. He's not a bit lazy, is he?" Then she looked up at me. "I don't know right off what chores Sheriff Leonard has in mind for you to do, but there can't be too many. You just go right on and see can you find someone to give you a job. You just go right ahead and leave Mr. Sheriff Dudley Leonard to me."

"Thank you, ma'am," I said, and I started toward the door. I turned back to say, "I'm thinking I'll just go out now and look for a job, if that's all right?"

"You do that," said Mrs. Leonard. She pointed to the grandfather clock in the corner. "Our cook, Mrs. Burns, likes to serve supper at six."

"I won't be late," I said.

I went down the stairs two at a time. I ain't claiming that I felt happy. Too much was hurting my insides, but outside the afternoon breeze felt good as it lifted the hair from my forehead. I didn't figure there was much hope, but I went first to the blacksmith's shop.

It took a minute for my eyes to adjust from the bright sun to the dim shop. I couldn't see old Elmer, but he called out a hello to me.

"Howdy," I answered, and I moved in the direction of the voice. Then I could see. Elmer had the same big bushy hair, and he had on his blacksmith's apron, but he wasn't working even a little bit. He was setting in a straight-backed chair, and across from him on a bench was a fellow I didn't know.

"Hey," Elmer said, "if it ain't Nobe Chase. Ain't seen you in a coon's age." He got up and slapped me on the back. "Sorry about your pa, boy," he added.

I nodded my head and sort of muttered a thank-you.

"Come to borrow my tools, did you?" Elmer asked.

"No," I said. "I come looking for work."

Elmer laughed. "Surely not here! Do I look like I need a helper, boy? Why, I've spent most of this day jawing at Wilson there." He shook his head. "Blasted motorcars! That's the problem, you know. More and more folks in these parts is buying 'em. Getting rid of perfectly good horses." He pounded his fist against his workbench. "At first, I said it was just a passing fancy. I said folks would lose their hankering after the motorcars, but it wasn't so." He shook his big bushy head again. "No, there sure ain't no call for me to be hiring on extra help."

"I figured so, but I thought I'd make sure. Thank you anyway." I turned to leave.

"You been over to the café?" the man called Wilson asked.

I whirled back. "No, you reckon I should go over there?" I practically yelled.

"Well," said Wilson, "I ain't saying they'll take you on or nothing, but I do know that Sim Harrison was saying as how his wife would need another dishwasher when the MKT crew hits town. He said they'd need another cook too, but you don't look like much of a cook."

"What's a MKT crew?" I asked.

"Railroad, you know, Missouri, Kansas, and Texas line. There's supposed to be a crew of workers coming in the next day or two, be around for a while putting in new rails. Sim and Daisy is figuring they got to eat, I reckon."

"Thanks," I said to Wilson. "Thanks a bunch." I turned to Elmer. "You too," I said. "Thanks for always being so good to me, letting me use your stuff."

"You want to thank me," Elmer said, "just don't be using your wages from that dishwashing job to buy no motorcar."

"I won't," I said, and I run out into the bright day again. Before I crossed the street to the café, I stopped to examine my hands and decided they was clean enough. It might be better, I thought, to take my cap off now, preventing any chance I'd forget to take it off when I got in the café. I didn't want my hair to look like Elmer's, so I went to the horse watering trough at the end of the street, dipped my hands into the water, and smoothed down my unruly curls.

My hand took to shaking when I went to reach for the door. I stuck my other hand in my pocket to touch the silver dollar. I wondered if Daisy Harrison would remember me from last winter. Maybe she wouldn't hire nobody who went around taking handouts.

The café had only one customer, an older man set eating a piece of pie. It looked like apple. My stomach started growling then, and I remembered that I hadn't had a thing to eat since the bite or two I got down of the oatmeal Ma had fixed me for breakfast.

When I pulled my eyes away from the pie, I seen the woman, who had come out from the kitchen. She was the same one from before. This time I noticed she was youngish, older than me but not as old as Ma. I noticed too that she was pretty, with nice thick black hair.

She asked me the same question as before. "You want to order?"

I shook my head. "I come to ask about work," I said. "I'm looking to find me a job." I gestured with my head to point back across the street. "Fellow over at the blacksmith shop said you might be taking on a dishwasher."

"That's so," said the woman. "Come on back to the kitchen, and we'll talk about it."

I followed her. In the kitchen was a big wood stove, a wooden icebox, and shelves with heavy white dishes. The woman set down at the small table where I had eaten the stew, and she motioned for me to take the other chair.

"What's your name?"

"Nobe Chase," I said, and I remembered to look her right directly in the eye. Ma always told me to look at folks when I talked to them.

"How old are you, Nobe Chase?" she asked.

"Fifteen, and a month, if a month counts."

"We count everything in the café business, you bet we do." She smiled at me then, and I sure did like that smile. It made me want to tell her the truth.

"I come in here last winter, most starved to death. You gave me stew." I held my breath, wondering if she'd still talk to me about working for her, but her smile didn't go away.

"I remember," she said. "I like helping folks when I can. You ever have a job before?"

"No, not what you'd call a job for pay." I looked at the calluses on my hands. "I worked plenty, though, you know, on our place. I'm a real hard worker."

"You say your name is Chase?"

"Yes, ma'am."

"Your daddy Melvin Chase that just died?"

"Yes, ma'am." I hesitated, then decided to go on. "I suspect you've heard of my pa, his drinking and all, but I hope you won't hold that against me. I ain't like that. I ain't nothing like my pa." I bit at my lower lip.

"Well, now, I reckon that's good. I heard you and your ma was moving in over at the sheriff's. That so?" She watched my face.

"We done moved in."

"You'd be handy to work then. What you think of the sheriff?"

I squirmed. "I reckon it'd not be fitting for me to speak ill of the man that took us in." I bit at my lower lip again. "My ma and me didn't have no other place to go."

"You don't like him, though. I can see that." She leaned closer to me from across the table. "Sheriff Leonard say it's okay for you to go to work?"

I nodded, and then I thought better of the nod. "Well, truth be told, it was Mrs. Leonard that said it was okay. I didn't ask the sheriff."

The woman laughed. "You done right," she said. "That man's so ornery, he'd say no just to bedevil you. Besides it's the missus that runs that household. Not many folks know that, Sheriff Leonard being such a tough-acting bag of wind, but he does exactly what his wife tells him to do in most cases." She nodded her head. "She's got the purse strings, that house, everything they have got passed down to her by her papa, and she manages it all, right along with the sheriff his ownself." She stood up. "The woman don't know what a bad man he is, though, her not getting out and all. I hope she don't ever find out, because she's a mighty fine person." She turned to go back into the front of the café.

"Wait, ma'am," I blurted out. "You never said. Do I get the job?"

She looked at me a long minute before she answered. "Well, we'll have to talk to my husband, Sim." She pointed to a small clock on the counter. "He'll be coming in about four with our little girl, but I reckon he'll agree with my opinion to hire you."

I could feel my face break into a big grin. "Oh, thank you, ma'am. You won't never be sorry. I promise you won't!"

"There's one more thing," she said. "We just hired us a man to cook alongside me. Lester Cotton's his name. He's colored, and he ain't none too easy to get along with, but he can cook like nobody I've ever seen. Do you reckon you can work with a cranky colored man?"

"I ain't one to pay no mind to color," I told her, "and I reckon living with Pa got me used to being fussed at."

"Well, that's good," she said, "on account if one of you has to go, it'd be you, hands down. Good cooks are lots harder to find than dishwashers." She turned back to the swinging doors.

"Wait," I said again. "I don't know what to call you." She looked back and smiled at me.

"You can call me Daisy like most folks do." She walked away, then looked back over her shoulder. "Oh, there's one more thing you ought to know. Dudley Leonard's my brother. I ain't proud of it, but it's a fact, just the same."

It was a shock. How could the sheriff have a sister as nice and pretty as Daisy? I touched the silver dollar in my pocket. Maybe my luck was changing some. I looked around the kitchen. What, I wondered, was I supposed to do until four o'clock? On the stove was a huge kettle of boiling water. On the worktable were two big dishpans and stacks of dirty dishes. Might as well get started, I told myself. With a big dipper, I took boiling water from the larger pan into the two dishpans. Next I added cold water from the pump, and I found the soap. By the time Daisy Harrison came back to the kitchen, I had washed all of the dishes and had them draining on a clean towel.

She carried two pieces of apple pie. "You've already gone to work," she said. "That's good." She put the pie on the table, went to the icebox, and took out a jug of milk. "Reckon you can take time to have a bite of pie with me?"

We was eating when the back door opened. A girl come running in. She was small, and her dark hair fell in thick curls around her face and down her back. "Mama, mama," she called. "I'm here." She ran to Daisy and threw her arms around her neck.

"I see you are," her mother said. She got up to go to the door and look out. "Did you bring your daddy?"

"He took old Roger over to the blacksmith's. Roger lost a shoe on the way into town." She stopped then and looked at me. "Who's he?" she half whispered to her mother.

"This is Nobe Chase," said her mother.

The little girl clapped her hands. "Oh," she said, "did he come to play with me?"

"No," said her mother. "He came to wash dishes."

The little girl came to lean against me like she had knowed

me all her life. I'd have thought it would make me feel uncomfortable, some strange kid pressed up against me. I ain't much used to being touched, but it didn't make me feel uneasy, not a bit. I can't say why, but I took to that little girl right off. She made me feel good inside.

"You might have some extra time, though," she said to me. "You might be able to play with me some."

"Lida Rose," Daisy said. "Nobe might not like being leaned on." She put out her hand and drew the little girl away from me. "Generally, it is better to get to know folks before you start leaning against them."

"Well, then," said the little girl, "it's okay." She moved back to lean on me. "I can lean on him for sure, because I know him. His name is Nobe Chase."

Chapter 4

I GOT BACK to the sheriff's house in time for dinner, which was cooked by a large lady named Mildred Burns, who left as soon as the last dish was taken from the stove. "I'm paid to cook," she told me and Ma, "not to serve or clean up. That'd be your job." She gathered her big bag, which I seen contained some potatoes and carrots from the sheriff's vegetable bin.

Ma noticed too. "Did you see them taters and such she had in that bag?" She shook her head. "That woman shouldn't be taking what don't belong to her."

"The way I see it, taking things from Sheriff Leonard ain't like stealing." I crossed my arms and leaned against the kitchen wall. "Taking things from that man is just a way of striking back at the meanest man that ever lived."

Ma shook her head. "Don't talk that way, son. Please don't talk that way or think that way. Thinking like that is bound to lead you into trouble."

"No, Ma, I ain't going to get in trouble, but I am going to get even. That man killed my dog, shot him just out of meanness. I can't let him get away with that."

"Sssh," Ma whispered. "Don't be talking like that so loud." She looked toward the kitchen door. "Was the sheriff to hear you, we'd likely be on the street." She put her hand on my cheek. "Please, son, I'm doing this for you same as for me. I'm sick of us having nothing."

My insides sort of softened up toward Ma. "I won't cause you no trouble, Ma," I promised, but even as the words come out of my mouth, I doubted if my words was true.

Supper was a pot roast with carrots and potatoes. I ate in the kitchen, but I helped Ma carry trays upstairs for her and the Leonards. "I got that job we talked about," I told Mrs. Leonard.

"Oh, my, how nice!" she said.

"There's work aplenty to be done right here," muttered the sheriff, but his wife shook her head.

"Let the boy be, Dudley. He's trying to better himself." She looked up at me. "Where will you be working dear?"

"Over at the café."

"That's lovely. You will be working for Daisy and Sim. Did you know Daisy is the sheriff's sister?"

"Half sister," the sheriff corrected.

"Well, yes, half sister. They had the same father." She smiled. "The little girl is a beauty. Did you meet Lida Rose?" She reached over to the table beside the bed and picked up a picture in a round gold frame.

"Yes, ma'am. I did meet her," I said.

Mrs. Leonard held the picture out for Ma and me to see. "This was taken when Lida Rose was just two," she said.

"She's precious," Ma said. I thought so too. Lida Rose had the same bright smile and curls in the picture.

Mrs. Leonard turned the picture back so she could study it. "Oh, I do love that little girl." She put the picture back on the table. "God never saw fit to make me a mother," she said. "I would have given anything to have a boy like you do, Vivian."

Ma reached out to pat Mrs. Leonard's hand. She must have felt me looking at her, because her eyes moved up to meet mine. I could see Ma was sorry for Mrs. Leonard, and I knew she must be feeling rotten about wanting to get in line to marry her husband when she died. Ma didn't look at me for more than half a second, just sort of bit at her lip and looked away. I went on down the stairs to eat.

At the kitchen table, I decided to think about nothing except the food. I told myself I'd quit worrying about what Ma does. I'd just eat the sheriff's food and wait for the chance to get even with him.

But that night it wasn't so easy to keep my mind off all that had happened. Laying there on my cot, I felt awful miserable. I didn't hear no coyotes howling off in the distance or no cows bawling for their calves. Most of all, I missed knowing old Rex was out under my window. I used to say good night to him when I blew out the lantern. He'd hear me even if the window was down, and he'd wag his tail. I could hear it thumping against the side of the house.

There was no one to see me, so I cried. I went to sleep that first night in the sheriff's house bawling into my pillow, and I got up even more determined to get even.

I was still thinking about revenge when I went to work. "The cook's back there," Daisy warned me when I come in. "Good luck," she added when I went through the swinging doors to the kitchen.

"My name's Nobe," I said to the tall black man bent over the stove.

"Don't much care what your name is, boy. Just care that

you stay out of my way." He flipped a pancake in the air. "Less I have to do with some sniffling white boy, the better I like it."

"Well," I said, "I'm not looking for no friends myself, so we ought to both be happy." I started up dipping dishwater from the huge kettle on the stove.

"Be a sight easier was you to pour the water out of that kettle into your pans," said Lester.

"Can't lift that kettle," I said. I didn't feel no shame. Wasn't nobody going to lift that kettle very easy.

"I reckon I can do it this once, if you don't go expecting it every time."

I looked at the man's thin arms and bent back. "I don't see as you look no stronger than me," I said.

Lester made a snorting noise. "Better look again, boy," he said. Then he lifted the huge kettle of water and moved easily with it to the worktable, where he filled the two dishpans. "Don't see as I'm no stronger than you, huh? Well, let me tell you something. There's a whole bunch ignorant white boys don't see."

I just took to washing dishes and didn't make no other comments, but Lester changed how I felt about my time in that kitchen. I was glad when my time for working was up.

After supper that night, I decided I'd walk out to see Mrs. Mitchell. I was used to seeing her at least three times a week when I'd deliver milk. Besides, I didn't want to spend an evening just setting around the sheriff's house.

I started down that familiar road, not minding at all walking through the spring evening. Preacher Jackson went by in his old truck. I didn't try to wave him down for a ride, but he stopped just past me and backed up.

My family never was much for churchgoing, and I didn't

expect the preacher to remember my name just from the burying, but he did. "Where you headed, Nobe?" he asked when I got into the truck.

"Out to see Mrs. Mitchell," I said. I wondered if I should say she was the teacher at the colored school and where she lived, but the preacher seemed to know. I guess he knows most everyone around.

"Going right past her place," he said. "You got business there?"

"I used to sell her milk," I explained. "Reckon I got kind of used to talking things over with her. Her son, Isaac, is just about the best friend I ever had, even if he is nine years older than me."

The preacher nodded his head. What he said next sure surprised me. "You're pretty good friends with Cinda Phillips too, aren't you?"

Cinda and her family never missed a service at the Last Chance Baptist Church, but still I couldn't figure how the preacher knew we was friends. "Yes, sir," I said. "We been friends since we started school." I looked over at the preacher. His face looked tired and thin. Folks say he's sickly, but he keeps working. He had a kind face, and I decided to ask him how he knew. "I am kind of wondering how you know me and Cinda are friends."

The preacher smiled. "Prayer," he said. For a minute I was real confused, but he went on. "Cinda asked the church to pray for you and your ma when your pa died."

"Oh," I said.

"You know, boy, it's good to have a friend who prays for you. It's just plain good to have friends, not much more important in this life than friends."

I opened my mouth then, and I couldn't believe what I heard myself saying. "Preacher," I said, "can I talk to you about something that troubles me powerful bad?"

"Reckon that's what preachers are for, boy."

"I been having impure thoughts." I blurted it out before I lost my nerve. "You know, about Cinda. I mean I been looking at her—" I lost my nerve. I just couldn't say breasts, not to a preacher. "I been thinking about her body." I put my face in my hands. "I reckon I'm headed to hell for sure."

The preacher laughed, a big full laugh. That surprised me. I dropped my hands and looked at him, mad that he'd laugh about me going to hell.

"I'm not laughing at you, son," he said. "I was just laughing about how every man ever breathed would be spending eternity in hell if thinking about a woman's body got him a ticket to damnation." He reached over and slapped at my shoulder. "Why, Nobe, you're just normal, that's all."

I was amazed! "You mean impure thoughts is okay?"

"Well, it's like this. You ought not to let such thoughts control you or take up too much time, but, boy, they are bound to come. Someday you'll marry, and you'll understand those thoughts better. I reckon we're made so that when a boy starts to be a man, he starts to think different. It's how God made us, and in the Good Book the Psalmist says, 'I will praise thee, for I am fearfully and wonderfully made.' There isn't any faulting how God made us."

I was still marveling over what the preacher had said when we drove past Cinda's place. I got a glimpse of her out in the garden behind the house. I knew she didn't see me, but I waved anyway because I was all filled up with lightness and wanted to do something.

I didn't have long, though, to celebrate the marvelous discovery. We drove past my old home place. I looked out into the twilight, and I sucked in my breath with surprise. I seen Pa out there. He was leaning against the barn, and I was standing beside him, sort of looking up at him. It was me all right, but not the same me that set in the preacher's truck. It was the little me, towheaded and about the size to start to school.

Ghosts? I wondered, but I knowed somehow that what I seen wasn't ghosts. What I seem come up from deep inside me, from an aching and a remembering. We drove on past our place, and I couldn't see them anymore, but the aching stayed.

Two automobiles set beside Mrs. Mitchell's house. There was her black Ford, and a shiny new red Nash touring car. "Wow!" I said, "The red one must be Isaac's. He bought his ma the black one last winter. He's got him a good job over in Tulsa at a bank."

"Sure enough?" Preacher Jackson sounded surprised. "I didn't know they were letting colored folks work in banks over in Tulsa now."

"It's a pure colored bank. They got lots of colored businesses over there. They call that part of town 'Black Wall Street,' whatever that means."

"Well, I'll be. Must be a good job all right to buy machines like those. How you getting home, Nobe?"

I shrugged. "Oh, I'll just walk. It's a nice evening for walking, I reckon."

"You be careful, now hear. Use your good horse sense when you're dealing with Sheriff Leonard. That one bears watching. He sure does."

"Thanks," I said, "Thanks for the ride, too. . . ." I hesitated, then went on. "Thanks for telling me about how God made us and all. I'm sure proud to know it."

"You let me know, should you have other things bearing on your mind," the preacher said, and he waved as he drove off.

Pa never did have any use for Preacher Jackson, but I decided I sure did. I guess Pa was wrong about the preacher, just like he was wrong about lots of other stuff.

I knocked at the door, and Mrs. Mitchell come to let me in. "Well, there you are, Noble. I've been wondering about you."

I explained about the ride with the preacher, and she urged me to come into the living room. "Isaac is here," she said. "You haven't had a real visit with him for a good bit."

Isaac was in his mother's rocking chair. He had on a blue shirt that looked new. His tall frame seemed to fill the room. His face was serious, and his eyes seemed almost sad until he smiled. That smile changed his face. "Hi, there," he said, and he punched my arm.

"Is that your car outside?" I said. "It's a beauty!"

"Yeah." Isaac sat back down and pointed for me to take a seat on the settee beside his mother. "I'm real proud of that car. Just bought it yesterday. I couldn't wait to get out here and show it to Mama. Want to drive it sometime?"

"Boy! Would I! But I don't have no idea how to drive no automobile."

Isaac laughed. "You didn't have any idea how to play marbles either, did you? You sure learned fast, though. How about you have your first lesson tonight?"

I just grinned. This was some evening, losing my fears over the impure thoughts and driving an automobile! "Gosh!" I said. "Gosh!"

Mrs. Mitchell got up. "May I get you a glass of tea, Noble? I've got ice in the icebox."

"Yes, ma'am, that would be nice," I said.

"And a sandwich? Are you hungry?"

"No, ma'am. For once, I've come to your house with a full stomach. I guess there is one thing good about living at the sheriff's place. Thank you, though, for asking and for all the times you fed me."

"It is always my pleasure to have you for a guest." She went to get the tea, but the house was small. I knowed she could hear me in the kitchen.

"Really, though, truth be told, there's something else good about living with the sheriff. I got me a job."

"Congratulations," said Isaac. "You'll be buying your own motorcar next."

I laughed. "No, I promised Elmer Keller at the blacksmith shop."

Mrs. Mitchell came back, gave me the tea, and settled on the settee, smoothing her cotton dress across her lap. "Oh, I'm pleased for you, Noble!" she said. "Where are you working?"

"At the café. I'm washing dishes."

"The café?" Mrs. Mitchell stood up, and her face seemed uneasy.

"Yes. I'm working for Daisy and Sim Harrison. They're paying me twenty cents for every hour I work. Ain't that amazing?"

Mrs. Mitchell had a strange look on her face. "It is amazing, Noble, but I thought you were going to work on not using 'ain't,'" she said.

"I am," I said. "I'll work on not saying 'ain't,' and I'll wash me a heap of dishes, every dish Lester puts in my stack."

"Lester?" said Isaac.

"Yeah, he's the cook they hired. He's colored, but he ain't—isn't—very nice. They say he can cook right well, though."

Isaac looked at his mother. "You knew Lester was back, didn't you, Mama?" he said. "I could see something bothered you about Nobe working at the café. I wish you had told me."

"I knew," said Mrs. Mitchell, and her face was troubled. "I've been putting off telling you." She sat down and turned to me. "Lester is indeed an unpleasant man, but he is Isaac's father and was once my husband. He comes back into our lives from time to time." She sighed. "I don't know why, because he has nothing but contempt for me and has done nothing for Isaac since he was little more than a baby." She smiled a forced little smile. "It would probably be best if you did not mention us to him, either. He would make your life harder, just because we are your friends."

I nodded. "I've had me lots of practice being around unpleasant folks. My pa wasn't exactly no Sunday school teacher. I reckon I can put up with Lester and maybe even the sheriff." I made my hands into fists. "I do hate that Sheriff Leonard, though. Hate him with a powerful, burning hate."

"No, Noble," Mrs. Mitchell leaned toward me. "Try not to hate. It's an emotion that eats away at those who allow it in their heart. Hatred does more harm to those who feel it than it does to those who are hated."

I looked down at flowers in the linoleum that covered the floor. "I'd do most anything for you, Mrs. Mitchell," I said, "but I can't stop hating the sheriff." I shook my head and bit at my lip. "That man killed my dog, shot Rex just to show how powerful he was. I hate him, all right, and I reckon I'm bound to get even."

"Oh, no," said Isaac, "not Rex! What happened?"

I told them all about it. "I buried him, though," I said when the story was done. "I couldn't just leave him there, like he said to do, not even if he had shot me." I looked at Mrs. Mitchell. "See why I hate him?" I said, and my voice almost broke into a sob.

Mrs. Mitchell reached out to pat my hand. "Oh, Noble," was all she said.

The room was quiet for a while. Then Isaac stood and walked to the side of the living room. "Look," he said. "See the Victrola I brought Mama." I'd seen it before, but I didn't let on because I knew Isaac was reaching for something we could discuss without anyone hurting. He started turning the handle, and music came out. Some fellow was singing about a place called Tipperary and about how it's a long long ways away.

After we had listened for a spell, I got up and said I ought to go. "I don't want to rile the sheriff by getting in late," I added. Then I looked at Isaac. "You can stay with your mama a while and give me a driving lesson later." I started toward the door, but Isaac stood up too.

"No, I've got to be getting back to Tulsa. We'll go together."

When we were outside, Isaac said, "Let me drive first. I want to talk to you. Then you can take the wheel."

Inside the automobile, I leaned back against the seat and rolled down the window. The May night air was cool and sweet with alfalfa growing nearby. I loved the feeling of the soft wind against my skin.

As soon as he had the engine going, Isaac started to talk. "Mama wouldn't like me telling you this," he said, "but for some reason, I feel like I want to tell you about Lester."

"Tell me," I said.

"Well, they lived in Atlanta. That's where I was born, and so was my brother, Daniel."

"You have a brother?"

"Had a brother. He died when he was four. I was two years younger. I wish I had been old enough to remember him. Mama and Lester were in school. He was almost finished and planning to go to medical school. I guess the man was brilliant once before his mind got eaten away." Isaac stopped, but I wanted to hear more.

"What happened?" I said, real quick.

"Well, Mama always looked up to Booker T. Washington. He was a colored man who believed education and hard work were the answer to our race's problems. Lester, though, took classes from a professor named Du Bois, who believed colored people had to speak out and fight for our rights. Lester started doing things Mama didn't approve of." He paused and took a deep breath. "She worked for a white family, and Lester would take care of us while she did. One day he left me with a neighbor and took Daniel out with him. There was a big construction job going on. Lester and his friends went down to the site to talk to the colored men, to urge them not to work for less than half what the white workers were being paid. Mama said the neighbor begged him to leave Daniel with her too, but Lester said, 'This is Daniel. He will be just fine in the lion's den.'" Isaac shook his head. "It didn't work like that, though. Things got ugly. White men started throwing rocks. Lester had Daniel in his arms, trying to shield him. A rock hit Daniel's head, though, and it killed him, right there."

"Gosh," I said, "that's awful."

"Yeah. Mama blamed Lester for taking Daniel there. I

imagine Lester blamed himself too, but all it did was turn him to alcohol and make him full of hate. They lived together for a while after that, but finally Mama couldn't stand it anymore. She took me, and we moved in with the people she worked for. They helped her finish school. She went back to using her maiden name, Mitchell, but with Mrs. because of having me. I've always used it too, but my real name is Cotton. He's no good, but Lester is my father, and I'm his son. Nothing can change that."

For a minute I didn't say nothing, but then I started talking about my father. "My pa wasn't no good either," I said. "He was a drunk and as mean as they come." I shrugged my shoulders. "But you know that. Everybody knows that!"

"Alcohol is one of Lester's demons too. I'd guess he's on the wagon now. That's when he usually shows up, during a dry spell." He sighed. "But alcohol is not his only problem, not even his biggest problem. There's hate too. That's what makes him so twisted. Lester's eaten up with hatred. He hates the entire white race, so be careful around him, Nobe."

"Thanks. I'll be careful." I looked out the window for a minute in silence, but then Isaac pulled the automobile off the road. We were in front of our old place, but it was too dark for me to really see anything. Still, though, the picture come busting into my mind. Pa was there in his old overalls. This time he was walking off through the pasture, and I could see little Nobe trotting after him, trying to catch up.

"Get out," Isaac said, "and come around here to try your hand at motorcar driving."

"I will," I said. "I want to in the worst way, but Isaac, you're a lot smarter than me, and since we both ended up with pas that ain't no good, maybe you can explain something to me."

"What?" said Isaac, "I'll tell you anything I can."

"Well, it's this. Why did I always hope Pa would love me?" My voice broke, and I swallowed back tears. "Pa treated me awful bad, and I guess most times I hated him for every time he ever hit me, and I hated him for every time he ever went off on a toot and left me and Ma hungry. Most of the time I hated him real good, but there was always times when I wished he would love me. I wished it until the day he died. I still wish he had. I wish he could of loved me just a little. What I want to know is why? Why didn't I just give up that silly wish a long time ago? That's what I want to know."

It was too dark for me to see Isaac's face, but I could tell by the sound of his voice that he was pretty near to crying too. "Well, Nobe," he said, "that story about fathers and sons is a real old one. It's even in the Bible about two brothers named Jacob and Esau. They both wanted their father's blessing real bad. I guess children always want their parent's love, but there's something about fathers and sons that's a little different. I guess boys just yearn to know their fathers care and are proud of us. I know I do."

"You do? You want to know that Lester fellow cares about you?"

"Yes. Oh, I would never say it to Mama, but yes, I'd like to hear him say, 'You did well, boy.'"

"He ain't never said it, huh?"

"No. He hasn't said anything to me in years. I suppose if he were to say anything now it would be something like, 'Trying to make yourself white, ain't you?'"

"I reckon someday I'll forget about Pa," I said.

"No, Nobe, I don't like to say it, but I don't think you're likely to forget. You aren't that kind of person. It will be a hole inside you, I think, all your life. But maybe good will come of that hole. Maybe you will work to fill it up with good things you do for other folks."

After that I got under the wheel. Isaac showed me how to start the car, and off we went down that bumpy road. A couple of times I like to have run right off the road. Isaac didn't yell none, even when he had to grab the wheel.

When we got to town, we didn't go straight to the sheriff's house. We drove around some, and I got pretty good at going around corners. I didn't run up on the sidewalk even once.

"You might not be ready for city driving yet, but you've done really well on your first lesson. I'll come and give you another one soon," Isaac said when I got out at the sheriff's place.

All that evening, when I was laying on my cot up on the third floor of that house, I was thinking about what Isaac said about the holes. He didn't say so, but I knew he had that same hole inside him. I finally decided I was maybe better off than Isaac because my business with Pa was done and over with. I knew for sure that I wasn't ever going to get Pa's blessing. If Isaac was right about me doing good things to fill up my hole, I could just get started filling it. Isaac, he was still hoping. Old Lester was no good at all. Wouldn't most people, white or colored, want nothing to do with him, but there was Isaac Mitchell with a fine education from a real college, a good job, and the fanciest motorcar I ever seen, but there he was still wanting old Lester's blessing.

I finally went to sleep while I was listening to a birdcall in the night. It was the same bird noise I used to hear at our place on spring nights. Most folks said it was a whippoorwill, but Pa always said it was a poorwill. He said we was too poor to have us a whippoorwill, and that our bird was its cousin, the poor relation named poorwill. I figured, laying there on the sheriff's cot, that the bird had followed me into town because he didn't want me to forget I was poor now that my stomach was full.

Ma woke me up early. "You need to help me with breakfast," she said. "The cook only comes in for supper. I'm supposed to fix morning and noon meals. You can help me this morning." Ma was real nervous. She kept pushing up on the piece of hair that slipped out of the knot she had put it up in. It pained me to see Ma so nervous because I knew it was Sheriff Leonard that made her that way. I wondered what it was that scared her most. Was she fretting because she might displease him, or was she afraid she might please him too much?

"Mighty fine breakfast, Viv," he said when he was wiping the egg off his face. His bug eyes had been following Ma all over the kitchen while he ate, and I wanted to pick up his plate and push the eggs right into his eyes. He was eating at the little table in the kitchen because his wife didn't wake up early for her breakfast, and of course, the sheriff had to get out and about to keep order in Wekiwa and the surrounding countryside. I smiled when I thought about it—Sheriff Dudley Leonard, the man of justice.

Ma let out a little sigh of relief when the sheriff left. "Things is working out good," she said. "Mavis Leonard is sure taking a shine to you, Nobe. She just might do some fine things for you, son."

I couldn't think about nothing except how much I hated that man. "Sheriff Leonard is as sorry as white dog manure," I

said, and I turned my back to Ma. It was one of Ma's own say-
ings, sorry as white dog manure. When I was younger I
thought she was throwing off on white dogs, saying they was
worthless, but later I figured it was the manure that was white
because it had been laying around a long time. I was glad it
wasn't white dogs, on account of Rex being white.

"Nobe," Ma said, "I wish you'd soften your heart some
toward the sheriff. We've got food in our stomach and a fine
house to live in. He's been mighty good to us."

"I don't call killing my dog being mighty good," I said, and
I went out the back door, slamming it after me.

"Make sure you get every weed out of them front flower
beds today, boy," he had told me at breakfast. "Mrs. Leonard
is mighty partial to them little petunias that grow there. I
paid good money to get old Roscoe Jones to plant them in
April, and she's real proud to have them up so early in the
year."

"It's been right warm this spring, ain't it?" Ma said. "Nobe
is good with flowers. He'll get every little thing out that ain't
suppose to be in that petunia bed."

I just stared at Ma. I had never known her to out-and-out
lie before. Me good with flowers! What would make her say
such a thing? We didn't ever have no flowers at our place.
We'd likely have had to eat them if we had. I started to say so
after the sheriff went out, but I didn't. I decided maybe she
was talking about how I liked to bring her wildflowers when I
was little. I didn't want to think as how the sheriff had turned
my ma into a liar.

Chapter 5

ALL MORNING I worked in the petunia bed. When I went inside once for a drink of water, I heard Ma and Mrs. Leonard upstairs.

"Wait, don't help me. I want to try." Even from downstairs, I could tell Mrs. Leonard was breathing hard. I climbed up the steps just far enough to see.

Ma stood just outside the bedroom door. Her body leaned in, and her arms were out. "Oh, Mavis," she said. "You might fall."

I moved more so that I could see around her. There was Mrs. Leonard, her arms outstretched, slowly inching one foot in front of the other. Her body weaved from side to side. I wanted to rush past Ma and help, but I could see that wouldn't be the thing to do.

After one step, Mrs. Leonard motioned for Ma. "Help me now," she said, and Ma was there in a flash, holding her up. I rushed across the width of the hall and into the room to take her other arm.

"Should I lift you?" I asked.

She shook her head. "No, dear." She stopped to breathe before she went on. "I want to try to walk more. I've got to build up my strength, can't let my heart and lungs get weaker and weaker, not if I want to live."

I looked at Ma. She looked right back at me, and I could see her swallow hard before she spoke. "You'll get stronger, Mavis," she said. "Me and Nobe will help you with your walking every day."

"We sure will," I said, and I smiled real big at Ma.

"Oh, I just knew it was a good idea to have you two move in here," said Mrs. Leonard, and she strained to move her right foot again.

"Yes," said Ma. "I reckon the good Lord knowed you and me could help each other." Her eyes looked damp, like she was fixing to cry.

We got Mrs. Leonard back in bed, and I went back out to the petunias, but when I went in for the noon meal, Ma told me that she had helped Mrs. Leonard with another walking session later in the morning.

"It's not Mavis's legs that give her the most problem," Ma said. "She had that awful infantile paralysis, left her heart and lungs weak. Mavis thinks with me to help she might be able to build up her strength." Ma took a loaf of bread from the oven. Then she turned back to me. "It's what I want, her getting stronger. You understand that, don't you, son?" She looked at me real close.

"Sure," I said. "I understand."

After I had me a bite of dinner, I went to work over at the restaurant. Lida Rose was in the kitchen, sitting on a high stool. Even though I liked the little girl, I wasn't much in the mood for messing with her or anyone else.

Her legs were too short to reach the floor, and her black patent leather shoes were dangling. When I came in, she held one foot out and said, "See my new socks. They got fluffles."

I looked at the sock. "You mean ruffles," I said.

She nodded. "Yeah," she said, "fluffles."

I didn't try to correct her again. "I got work to do," I said.

She shook her head again. "That's what Mama said. She said I shouldn't talk to you too much 'cause you got work to do. She sent me back here 'cause I wanted to talk to the customers. I don't know why I can't talk to them. They don't got work to do. They're just eating. Eating ain't work, but Mama said I couldn't talk to them."

I dipped out hot water for the dishpan. "You talk a lot," I said.

She shrugged her shoulders. "If you don't want me to talk so much, you could play with me. That would keep me from talking so much, I bet."

I just kept on stacking dirty dishes in the pan. She reached out and pulled at my overalls. I turned to look at her. "See this here pan of dishes," I said, aggravated like. "They sure ain't going to wash their own self while I'm playing dollies or something with you."

She stared up at me, and her lips started to quiver like she was fixing to cry. "I didn't say we had to play with dolls," she protested. "We could play I Spy right here while you do them dishes."

"I don't know how to play that game," I lied. "You'd just as well give up on me and find something else to do."

She ignored me. "When you play I Spy, you pick out something." She stopped and looked around the kitchen. "Like that rooster on the calendar." She pointed to the calendar on the wall. "Then you say, 'I spy with my little eye something brown and yellow with some red on it.' Then you get three guesses. If you don't guess, I tell you, and I win that time. Then it's your turn." She nodded her head a couple of times, all satisfied and pleased with herself about the instructions she had given me. "You can go first, since you're just learning," she said.

I looked around until I decided on a big iron skillet that set on the stove. "I spy something round and black," I said.

"That ain't right," she said. "You left out the part about your little eye."

"My eye ain't little, though," I protested, but she shook her head.

"How many are you?" she asked.

For just a second, I didn't know what she was talking about. I started to say, How many what am I, but then I realized she meant how old. "Fifteen," I said.

"Is that a grown-up?" she asked.

"Not exactly," I said, "but I ain't no kid either."

"You got to say, 'with my little eye.' It's a rule."

"All right. All right." I kept right on washing the dishes. "I spy with my little eye something round and black."

"Is it that big fry skillet?" she asked.

"That's right," I said. Just then Lester came through the back door, and I told him hello.

"I ain't interested in carrying on no conversations," he muttered. Then his eyes fell on Lida Rose. "And I'm one black person ain't interested in being no nursemaid to no little white child. You skeedaddle." He waved his arms at her like he was shooing chickens or something.

Lida Rose jumped down from her stool. She looked real afraid, and I thought sure she would turn tail and run, but she didn't. She pushed out her lip and crossed her arms. "I ain't going to skeedaddle," she said. Then she leaned her face over as close to the man as she could get without moving. "And you don't know your colors very good," she told him. "I ain't white. I'm pink." She held out her arm to show, "Besides that, you ain't even black. You're more brown. Every single five-year-old I know can call out the names of colors. You ought to be ashamed."

"Out," thundered Lester. "You go tell your mama that I won't work in here if you stay."

Lida Rose scooted toward the door and disappeared out into the café. I turned back to my dishes. "She ain't a bad kid," I said.

Lester looked at me real hateful, and he made some sort of huffing sound. "Don't need your comments, neither," he said. "Like you know a solitary thing about children." He turned back to his work.

"Reckon I know 'bout as much as you do." I had me an idea then. "You got children of your own, do you?" I just wondered if he would tell me the truth. I wondered if he would own up to being Isaac's pa. I wondered if my own pa would have claimed me.

"Ain't none of your business, that's what I know. You've got no call asking do I have me a son or not."

"Never said a word about sons," I muttered, and I went back to washing dishes.

We worked without talk for about an hour. I never looked

at Lester even once, just washed my dishes like I was the only person in the room. I guess he forgot about me too because he started to sing, low and sort of under his breath. He sang, "Swing low, sweet chariot, coming for to carry me home." I liked hearing him sing, liked it so much that I felt uncomfortable. I knew Lester wasn't singing for me. I knew it would make him mad for me to be appreciating the song, and I made sure I didn't look at him.

Lida Rose stayed in the front with her mama for about an hour. Then she come busting through the swinging door. "Nobe," she yelled, "your girlfriend's here, and Mama said you can take a break and come eat with her."

Lester stopped singing and looked at me. There was a snarl on his face, and I knew he was mad because I was taking a break. I could imagine him saying, "Sure, the white kid gets paid to flap his gums with a girl while the colored man's working in the hot kitchen."

I didn't know what to do, but I looked up to see Daisy Harrison in the doorway. "Come on out, Nobe," she said. "Cinda is here to see you. I told her you could take a break and have a piece of pie with her."

Lester slammed down a skillet on the stove. Daisy turned to him. "Would you like a piece of pie, Lester?"

"Not to eat in this hot kitchen," he muttered.

"You could take it out and set on the back porch. There's a bit of breeze out there."

"No," said Lester, and he went right on working.

"Why can't Lester eat in front, Mama?" Lida Rose asked, and the room was real quiet. I looked at Daisy waiting for an answer. Lester didn't turn away from the stove, but I could feel him waiting too.

"Well, sugar," Daisy said. "I wouldn't mind to have Lester in front, but some of our customers would." She shook her head. "Some things ain't right, but we got to go along with them because of the customers."

"Why?" asked Lida Rose. "Why would the customers care about Lester having a piece of pie."

"Because I'm colored," Lester muttered. "White folks think they're way too good to eat in a room with a man like me."

"Ma," said the little girl. "Is that true? Do folks not want to eat with Lester just because he's brown?"

Lester didn't wait for Daisy to answer. "Little girl," he said, "I am telling you, I ain't brown, I'm black."

"Well," she said, "the whole thing don't make sense to me." Her mother reached out and pulled at her arm until Lida Rose followed through the restaurant door. I went after them.

Cinda was there at a table by the window. I caught my breath when I saw her because she looked so beautiful. The light was shining on her red hair, and it looked like it was on fire. Her face looked peaceful and sweet, like I figured an angel's would look. Suddenly, I felt afraid to go over to her. Cinda had changed on me. She was just plain too beautiful to be a friend of mine, but she looked up at me and smiled just like she'd been doing since we was six years old.

"Hey, Nobe, there you are." She motioned for me to come to the table. "I'm so glad you've got yourself a job, and look, Daisy put out a piece of pie for you."

For just a minute, I couldn't move or say a word. I had to sort of give my mind a shake and tell myself that this was the same old Cinda. Finally, I said, "Oh, boy, that looks good." Then I got the idea she might think I was talking about her and being fresh, so I said, "The pie, that's what looks good."

"It sure does," she said, and she started to eat hers, but between bites she kept talking. "Boy, do I have news for you. Something real exciting is fixing to happen around here for a change."

I settled myself across from her, but I kept my eyes glued right to the pie. It scared me too much to look at Cinda, because I couldn't get my mind on to any news, no matter how exciting. All I wanted to think about was Cinda, and I wanted to touch her too. Them same old impure thoughts went to coming to my mind. I'd been feeling better about them thoughts since my talk with Preacher Jackson, but I didn't want to give in to them with Cinda setting right there in front of me. I sure wouldn't be able to talk with them thoughts in my head.

"Nobe Chase," she said, "are you listening to me a'tall?"

"Huh?" I said. "Sure I was listening."

"What did I say?" she demanded.

"You said your pie was good," I said real serious like, but suddenly I realized she must have said something else after that.

"I said one of them barnstormer fellows is in town," she said. "His name is Basil Bailey. He's the main pilot, but a fellow named Willie something flies while Basil does tricks on the wing of the plane.

"They're going to land out in Widow Carter's pasture. They say Basil's a friend of Olly's, you know, the widow's brother who ain't right in the head because of the war, shell-shocked. That's what they call it. Well, Basil was a pilot in the war with Olly, and I reckon he feels real bad about the shell shock and all." She stopped to take a big breath. "He does all kinds of tricks, gets out on the wing while the other fellow flies. He takes folks up on rides for five dollars." I never had ever seen Cinda so fired up about anything. Her eyes were blazing like a fire in a fireplace.

"Five dollars," I said. "That's a lot of money. I ain't been paid yet." I shrugged my shoulders. "Even if I had done got my pay, I wouldn't have that kind of money."

"Oh, I never thought you would! Land's sake! I wouldn't feel right about throwing that much money away just for a thrill, anyway, but we can see the tricks. How much longer you got to work?"

I shrugged my shoulders. "I got a pile of dishes in there from noon. This place was busting with railroad guys."

"Well, come on." She put the last bite of pie in her mouth. "I'll help you."

I stood up, but I didn't move. "I don't know," I said. I was doubtful that I could keep from dropping the dishes with Cinda standing in there beside me. "It's awful hot in there, and Daisy might not like me having help."

Cinda shook her head. "Daisy won't mind, and you know I worked hot before." She reached out and grabbed my hand. "Hurry!"

She pulled me after her. I opened my mouth to warn her about Lester, who was baking for tomorrow, but it was too late. We was in the kitchen, and Lester was glaring at us, his face all twisted into an ugly expression.

"Who's she?" He used his head to point to Cinda.

"This is my friend, Cinda," I said, "and she's going to help me do these dishes."

"Just like some puny white boy, getting a girl to do your work."

I opened my mouth to say something to him, but I didn't get a chance. Cinda was already talking. "Look, here, mister," she said. "I don't know why you're up on your high horse just because I want to help Nobe a little. Me and him are friends, and friends help each other. Seems like a man your age would know all about that." She turned to me. "Let me wash. I'm fast. You dry."

We made quick work of them dishes, and then we went scooting out the back door. It was two miles to Widow Carter's place. We hoped someone would come along to give us a ride, because if we had to walk all the way, we might not be there to see the plane come in.

Sure enough Preacher Jackson came along in his truck. The preacher has to work at different things too besides preaching because he has a bunch of kids, and I guess preaching don't pay real well. During the winter, he cuts down trees and sells firewood to folks who don't want to cut it theirselves. In summer, if he's able, he works in the fields, baling hay and doing whatever else he can.

First he went right on by us, and that made Cinda real mad. "You'd think a man of God would take pity on folks trying to see an airplane!" she said.

But the preacher stopped just a ways down the road. "I reckon he didn't see us right off," I said.

"Want a lift?" he yelled, and we ran up to climb in the back of the truck. He had his wife and two or three little kids in the front. A girl who looked about ten and a boy just a little older were in the back.

"Hi, Cinda," the girl said. The preacher's kids know Cinda on account of her and her folks going to church every Sunday.

Cinda said hello, and we climbed in back. The boy didn't

say a word, just stared off to the side of the road like he was watching for something. The girl was real interested in us, though. "What's your name?" she said to me.

"Nobe Chase," I said. "What's yours?"

"Puddin' Tane," she said, "ask me again, and I'll tell you the same."

"Her name's Mildred," Cinda said.

Mildred turned her attention to Cinda. "Is Nobe your beau?" she asked.

Cinda's face turned as red as her hair. "He most certainly is not," she said. "Me and Nobe, we've been friends since we first started to school. We like to sort of hang around with each other, that's all."

I sort of looked down because, of course, I *was* wanting to be Cinda's beau. It seemed like, though, the thought never crossed her mind. Maybe if a fellow and a girl have been friends since they lost their first teeth, the rules can't change after all that time. I was sure wishing they could.

The Jacksons was going to Widow Carter's just like me and Cinda was. I was kind of surprised that a preacher would want to see a barnstormer, but he was real excited about it.

Cinda and me thanked the preacher for the ride, and we raced off across the pasture to where a crowd had already gathered. We had just got to the crowd when someone yelled, "Look!"

We did, and there was the plane. It buzzed down so low over Widow Carter's barn that the crowd made an "ah" sound almost all at once, like we was just one big person instead of a whole bunch of different people.

"They'll go up again now and do some stunts," a fellow behind us said, and he was right. When they were back above the barn again, the plane started to circle. Me and Cinda kept our eyes on it, and we almost held our breath. Then one man climbed out on the wing, and we really were afraid to breathe. When he was just barely on the wing he leaned back, and the pilot handed him a baseball bat and a small bag. With the bat under his arm, he stood up on the wing.

"There'll be a ball in that bag, sure as you're alive," said the man behind us, and sure enough he was right again. The man on the airplane opened the paper bag, took out a red ball, and let the bag go in the wind. Then he held the ball up in front of the bat, dropped it, and hit it hard. The crowd went wild, but I didn't spend any time clapping or shouting.

"I'm going to go find that ball," I told Cinda, and I tore off in the direction it had landed. Cinda came right along. We didn't pay any mind to the stunts even though the crowd was oohing and aahing. When we got to the general area where we thought the ball had come down, we split up and looked for it.

Pretty soon Cinda yelled, "Here it is," and she held it up for me to see. The stunts were over now, and by the time we ran back to the crowd, Basil and Willie was landing. Cinda and I stood near the edge of the up-front group.

Both men came climbing out of the plane, and the crowd went to cheering real loud. First Basil and Willie walked to the widow and her brother, who were standing in the front of the crowd. Willie shook Olly's hand, and Basil gave him a big hug. The crowd cheered again, and I expected Olly to bolt and run on account of him being so shy, but he didn't.

The flyers went back to the plane, and Basil climbed back up on the wing. Then he started to yell out, "Who wants a ride? Only five bucks for the ride of your life! I can take three at a time, folks, because Willie here wants to stay on the ground and look for him a gal. Me, I'm a married man, so I can keep my mind on the flying. Now who will be first?"

No one stepped up. "Come on," shouted Basil. "Don't be nervous about going up! Why, I tell you what I'll do! You give Willie here the five dollars, and if we crash and you get killed, you can have your money back!"

The crowd laughed, but no one stepped up to buy a ride. Cinda still had the ball in her hand. "Go give the ball to Basil," I said to her.

"I sort of thought I'd keep it, you know, as a souvenir." She turned the ball over in her hands. "I don't reckon they know we've got it, and I bet they've got another one."

I shrugged my shoulders. "Well, I was thinking they might give you a free ride if you was to give it back to them."

Cinda sucked in her breath. "Oh, do you think so?"

"It's worth a try," I said.

Cinda stepped toward Basil, but she grabbed my hand and sort of pulled me after her. When we was close to him, he said, "You two want rides?"

Cinda shook her head no. "We ain't got no money," she said. "But here's your ball we found."

"Well, now, that's real neighborly of you, bringing back my ball. I'm real fond of that particular ball." He took the ball and held it up for everyone to see. "This here young lady brought back my ball," he yelled. "I figure maybe she ought to get a free ride."

"Sure thing," yelled Willie. "You climb right on up there, darling."

Cinda didn't move. "It was Nobe's idea," she said. "I never would of thought to go look for the ball, but right off that's what he thought of. Nobe ought to be the one to get the ride instead of me."

"No," I said. "You found it fair and square. You go."

"Well, looks like we've got us a pair here, huh, Willie?" he called. "It appears we'll have to take them both."

Cinda squeezed my hand so hard I thought she might break my fingers off, but she dropped my hand real quick when Basil said, "Climb on in." She was up in that plane in nothing flat, like she'd been scrambling up into airplanes for all her life. Basil Bailey pointed us to the backseat.

About the time we got settled, Preacher Jackson joined us, and Basil started up the engine. My stomach felt real strange when we took off, and I reckon I was holding my breath pretty tight. Cinda grabbed my hand. Her fingernails were cutting into my skin, but I didn't try to get loose. It wouldn't have done me any good to try anyway. Cinda wouldn't have let go of that hand no matter what.

As soon as we was off the ground, the preacher started shouting out a prayer so loud you'd think he thought God had to hear him over the roar of the airplane. "Oh, Lord," he prayed, "forgive me my sins. You know I started swearing a blue streak this morning when that old cow took to kicking me because I forgot to put the kicker chains on her. And forgive me for being so interested in worldly things as to make me spend five dollars on this ride. And dear, God, if you can see your way to spare our lives, I'll be a better man, and Lord, I think Nobe, who is in the backseat, will be a better man, too."

I wanted to say to the preacher that God sure ought to know who it was in the backseat without being told. I also wanted to say I wasn't making any promises about being a better man. Not that I wouldn't like to do better, but see, Cinda was leaning against me while she held on to my hand with one hand and clutched my knee with the other. There I was up above the world, where any fool would have his mind on dying and trying to get into heaven. Not me, though. I started having impure thoughts right there in that airplane. I reckon I would have impure thoughts even if one of them clouds parted and I was to see the face of God. I reckon I've just got one of them kind of minds. I just had to hope God knew what it was like to be a boy who tried to keep a pure mind, but just couldn't.

"This is as high as we go, folks," Basil yelled. I was too scared to look down until then, and I just had to look. Boy howdy! I never had any notion how beautiful our plain old Oklahoma really was. I could see the widow's barn, and her pretty fields of corn and wheat. One field had just been plowed, and the brown looked so pretty there in the middle of the growing things. Over in her pasture, two jersey cows was standing in a pond so as to cool off. The cows was real small from up there, but they looked so beautiful. I could see Wekiwa over to my left. For a minute I didn't think it was our town on account of how pretty it was, but then I looked at the lay of the buildings, the bank building on one corner being the tallest and all. I knew for sure it was Wekiwa.

The funny thing is that I stopped having them impure thoughts, and I went to talking to God too, not out loud like the preacher, but just quiet inside my head. I told him that I never did know how beautiful his world was, and I sort of thanked him for letting me live in it.

I think Cinda was feeling the same way. "Oh, Nobe," she said. "Just look down there. The world's so wonderful and so big. It's just so big, and I want to see it, Nobe, I want to see it all, Noble. Oh I do."

We started down then, and we buzzed real low over that barn again. When we landed, Basil said, "I hope you three will urge the others to go up too. We'd like to make some money today."

"I surely will do that," Preacher Jackson said, but when we stopped, he didn't get much of a chance.

Even before Basil Bailey had a chance to get out, Cinda popped out of that seat. Quick as a wink, she was up on the back of that plane. "You got to go up," she yelled. "Even if you've got to get a mortgage on your farm to do it, you've got to go up. There ain't nothing like seeing our world from way up there, the way God sees it."

We climbed out of the plane then. People was crowding up to pay their five dollars. Cinda and I pushed our way through the crowd to stand up and watch. Then she did the most amazing thing. She leaned right over and kissed me. The kiss landed half on the side of my lips and half on my chin. "Thank you, Nobe," she said. "If you hadn't thought of getting that ball, we might never have had a chance to see." I felt like I was purely flying again!

Chapter 6

I JUST NEVER DID FEEL the same inside after we went up in that airplane with Basil Bailey. I'd walk around Wekiwa looking at things like the street or the blacksmith shop, and I got to studying about how pretty things looked from up there. And then, of course, there was that kiss. I spent me some real nice times thinking about that kiss.

Sure. I had not forgot what Cinda said about me not being her beau. But that kiss was real, and it was her idea. There was flyers around town about how Basil was aiming to be back in town on June 2. I'd have me a payday by then, and I knew what I'd do with the money. I forgot all about saving for my escape. I'd use the money for an airplane ride for Cinda. I might ask Daisy about an advance on my wages, so that I'd have enough for me too.

It had been three days since the ride, and I was still feeling like I was walking in high cotton. The café was open late on the last night of May because it was Tuesday, and the railroad men always came in for supper on Tuesday night.

As soon as I got out the front door of the sheriff's house, I started to whistle, "You Are My Sunshine." Most times I went around to the back door of the restaurant, but I just went in the front, sort of wanting to see the folks who were eating from the dishes I'd be washing in a few minutes.

My whistling stopped when I opened the front door and saw Sheriff Leonard. He had been at his house having his supper with Mrs. Leonard just a few minutes earlier, but now he was having pie while Charlie Carson from the bank ate roast beef. There was another man with them, but I didn't know him.

I just nodded to Daisy and was about to go through the swinging doors when Preacher Jackson busted through the front doors. His face was red, and his hair was wild.

"War's broke out in Tulsa!" he yelled, and he leaned against the counter like he'd run the whole twelve miles from there.

"Mercy," said Daisy. "Don't tell us the Germans have attacked Tulsa!"

The preacher shook his head, but he didn't say anything for a minute, just breathed heavy. Finally he was able to talk. "It wasn't the Germans," he said. "It's the colored people and the white people fighting each other. They're burning the town."

Sheriff Leonard jumped up, and he had his hand on his gun. "The damn coloreds are setting fire to Tulsa?" he yelled.

"No," said the preacher. "It's the whites that are doing the burning."

"Well," said the sheriff, "they're bound to have good reason. The coloreds must of got out of hand, else the whites wouldn't have to put them in their place."

The preacher wiped his face with a bandanna. "I was there when it started. A colored boy was arrested yesterday because a white woman claimed he grabbed her in the elevator where she worked. The newspaper had an article that got people to saying the boy ought to be lynched."

Daisy brought the preacher a glass of iced tea, and he took a big drink before he went on. "Well, sir, a crowd of white men gathered down by the jail, talking up the lynching. Then the coloreds, they start to gather too, wanting to protect the boy." He wiped his hand across his eyes. "There was some of us, both white and colored, who were a trying to calm people down. I was standing right where the whole thing started, could have reached out to touch the fellow that got killed. That's exactly what I should have done, should have reached out to stop him." He stopped to get another drink. I noticed how his hand shook, holding the glass.

"What happened?" Banker Carson was up by then, and he pulled at the preacher's arm.

"Well, sir," said the preacher, "there was this colored fellow had a gun, and the white man said, 'What are you doing with that gun?' The colored man, he says, 'I'm fixing to use it if I have to.' The white man says, 'No, you're not,' and right off he starts to wrestle the colored man for the gun. The gun goes off, and the white man falls right there at my feet, dead. The shooting starts then. I ran." A terrible wounded look come across his face, and I was afraid he might start to cry, but he went on. "What was I to do? I couldn't talk sense to men who were shooting at one another. They brought in a truckload of white fellows with guns, gasoline, and matches. They started burning everything in sight! Churches! They even burned churches." He shook his head, and despair seemed to take over his whole body. He sort of fell into a chair near the counter. "Why would they burn churches? I never thought I'd see the day!"

Sheriff Leonard pulled himself up to stand real tall. "Reckon I'd better be rounding up me some deputies," he said. "The coloreds could be attacking us next, but we'll be ready."

The preacher lifted his head. "Didn't you hear anything I said, man?" he asked. "It's the whites that are doing the attacking, burning homes with women and children right there inside. It's a shameful day," he said, "a shameful day." He put his head back down.

"Little children," said Daisy, "little children like Lida Rose seeing such awful things." She went over to put her hand on the preacher's shoulder.

Sheriff Leonard wasn't satisfied. "I don't know," he said. "Seems to me like we ought to be taking precautions against trouble." He folded his arms across his chest, and his red face seemed lost in thought.

"Dudley," Charlie Carson said, "what do you think is about to happen here in Wekiwa? We don't have a colored family here in town. Now we do have a few families out south of town, nice, peaceful folks they are. You think they're likely to go crazy and start a war, do you?"

"A lawman's got to be ready," said the sheriff. "You can't never tell what the coloreds will do if they get all hot under the collar. I'm getting some men together."

"Sit down, Dudley!" said Charlie Carson. He hit the table he stood beside with his fist. "I'm telling you, you are not deputizing a bunch of fools and starting some kind of trouble here."

I never knew anyone had the nerve to talk to Sheriff Leonard that way, but he took it. Charlie Carson pulled back a chair, and the sheriff set down in it. Then Mr. Carson set down across from him. When he talked next, his voice was quieter. "Think about it, Dudley. You get a bunch of guys together with guns, and there's bound to be trouble. The preacher just told us what happened in Tulsa on account of hotheads."

Daisy was still looking at Preacher Jackson. "Could I get you a plate of food, Brother Jackson?" she asked. "It would be on the house, of course."

The preacher raised his head. "That's kind, but thank you, no." He wiped at his face again. "I couldn't eat a bite." He put his head back down. "I should have stayed," he said, real soft. "That's the thing that's eating at me. I should have stayed. Maybe there was some little thing I could have done, some little thing to help those suffering people. All I did was run. I started up my truck, and I got out of there fast as I could." He looked right at me then. "Most any man would have stayed and tried to help."

"No." I shook my head. "I suspect most any fellow would have done what you did. You got a wife and kids to think about too, Preacher. What would have happened to your wife and kids was you to get yourself shot or burned up in Tulsa?"

The preacher didn't say anything. He just stared at me like he wasn't sure where I had come from or who I was. "Nobe," said Daisy, "why don't you see Brother Jackson home?"

It was just a block over to the church, and the preacher lived right next door. "Sure," I said. I took hold of the preacher's arm. "I'll walk with you." I helped him up, but he seemed sort of shaky on his feet. I didn't figure he could walk even to his house. "Is your truck out front?" I asked.

He looked at me, sort of dazed like. "Yes, I believe it is. Yes, I must have driven it back from Tulsa."

"Come on." I steered him toward the door. I did not look at Sheriff Leonard. Somehow I just plumb could not stand to see that man's face one more time that night.

I was helping the preacher into the car when he pointed off to the east. "See the flames?" he said. "The flames of hatred. God forgive us," he whispered.

I looked back to the east, and sure enough, I could see the light in the darkness. "I am right glad I ain't in Tulsa tonight," I said, and it was just that second that I thought of Isaac Mitchell.

The preacher thought of Isaac too. Before I could ask about him, the preacher started to talk. "Isaac Mitchell was there. Trying to talk his people into going home, saying the law would protect the colored boy. He wanted to get both sides to just go home." His voice broke. "I saw them strike him with the butt of a shot gun. I saw him fall, but he got up." He shook his head. "I believe I saw him get up. No, I can't be sure. Isaac may well be dead by now. He was such a good young man, a blessing to his dear mother."

My heart took to thumping like it was fixing to break out of my chest. I looked again at the bright spot on the night horizon. Tulsa was on fire, and Isaac was there. He was there, and he was injured.

I shoved the preacher in and fired up the truck. Driving that old truck wasn't as easy as Isaac's new automobile. At first I had trouble keeping it on the street. I remembered how Isaac had said I wasn't exactly ready for city driving, but it sure looked like I would be driving in a city. By the time I had it headed down the preacher's street, I had my mind made up. "Preacher," I said. "Can I borrow your truck? I got to go to Tulsa. I got to try to find Isaac and bring him home."

"Oh, my boy," he said. "It won't work. I tried to turn back. After I came to myself, I tried to turn back for that very reason. No, they won't let you in. The National Guard has that part of downtown blocked off."

"I've got to try," I said.

"Well, then, turn the truck. I'll go with you. You've got to have help."

"No, Preacher," I said. "You're done in for tonight. I can get me someone else to help." While I was saying that, I knew who I'd get. Lester. He was my only choice.

At the preacher's house, I didn't even turn off the truck, just helped the preacher to the door, hurrying him as much as I could. Then I ran back to the truck and jumped in. I was afraid Lester would be leaving the café, and I didn't have no idea in the world where the man slept at night.

I was just about to get back in the truck when the preacher's wife came running after me. "Edwin says take this blanket and the water." She pushed a blanket and a jug at me. For just a minute I wondered who Edwin was. I had never heard anyone call the preacher that before, but I reckon he had to have a given name. It wasn't likely that his ma and pa called him "preacher" when he was born, or that his teacher said "Brother Jackson" when she wanted him to recite.

I got back to the café just in time. Lester was just reaching for his old felt hat when I busted through the back door. "Don't leave," I shouted. Then I remembered the sheriff was likely still out front. I lowered my voice. "You've got to go with me," I said, "but we can't let anyone know."

"I ain't going nowhere with some crazy white boy in the middle of the night." He shoved me away from the door and started out it.

"Please," I begged. "It's for Isaac. It's for your son. He needs us."

He whirled back, and his face was full of hate. "What are you talking about? I ain't got me no son. You just ask his mama. She'll tell you. I got one boy killed, and she took the other one away from me. I ain't got no son."

I didn't know what to say to that, so I ignored the comment. "Step outside with me," I said, "and I'll show you Tulsa burning."

"Huh?" he said, but he stepped out, and I followed him.

I pointed to the east. "See that glow. That's Black Wall Street. That's where Isaac works and lives. There's been trouble between the coloreds and the whites, and the whites are burning out the whole colored section. The preacher was there. He seen it all start, and he seen Isaac get hit hard with a gun."

Lester made some sort of sound way down deep in his throat. "Will you come with me?" I said. "I'm driving the preacher's truck." He didn't answer me, just headed for the truck.

I wondered what it would be like driving through the night with Lester beside me. I wondered if he would talk, but he didn't. We drove that whole twelve miles without a word passing between us. Lester just set over there, hating me. I could feel him hating me like I was the one that hurt his son instead of the one trying to help. I wanted to ask why, but I didn't. I just figured hate like Lester's couldn't ever be shrunk down to words.

The glow in the sky got brighter and brighter as we got closer to Tulsa. My fear got brighter and brighter too. Finally Lester said something, but what he said didn't make me feel any better. He said, "I reckon this is the night I kill me some whitey. It's a thing I've known was coming my whole life."

I figured Lester was just as likely to pick me to be his dead whitey as any other fellow, but I just kept driving. I did start to wonder if maybe I'd made a mistake. Maybe I'd have been smarter to bring along poor addled Preacher Jackson than this hate-filled colored man.

We didn't get far into Tulsa when we saw the roadblock ahead. "Get down in the floorboard," I told Lester, "and put that blanket over you. They won't let me through with you in the car."

I was plum amazed to see Lester dropping down. I never had any real notion that he would do a thing I asked him to. I slowed down the truck when I saw a soldier holding up his hand. "Stop," he shouted, and I did. He walked over to my window. "No access to this area." He pointed back toward the way I had come. "You've got to turn around."

My mind was spinning. I should have thought of something to say on the ride, but somehow I had just got all caught up in Lester and not really done any planning. Mama, I thought. Pert near everybody had a mama somewhere, and pert near everybody loved their mama. "It's my mama," I said. "She went down to visit a colored woman." I took a breath and thought I'd better explain why my saintly mama went down to colored town at night. "See, this here woman is sick, and she's got a passel of kids"—I looked down at the black bundle in the floor—"and she's got a no-good husband," I added. "Anyway, Mama went before the trouble started, and we ain't seen hide nor hair of her since. My little sister, she's crying up a storm."

"Well," said the soldier. "I don't like letting a kid like you through. I doubt your judgment's as good as a grown man's. Say, don't you have a daddy?"

"Why, yes," I said. "But my pa's in the National Guard, so of course, he got called up just like you did. He don't know Mama hasn't made it home, or he'd be worried sick. Maybe you know him—Melvin Chase," I said. "He's a big fellow with a black beard."

"Can't say I do." The soldier scratched his chin. "Do you know where this colored woman lives, just exactly?"

"Yes, sir," I said. "Don't know as I could come up with an address exactly, but I can drive there quick as a wink."

"You get your mama, and you skedaddle out of that mess." He waved me on.

"Much obliged," I yelled as I drove off. Lester popped up right off. "I think you ought to stay down," I said, but Lester was done taking my advice.

We made it through a couple of blocks without any trouble, but then we saw a line of men stretched across the street in front of us.

"Don't slow down," Lester said. "They'll move all right as soon as they see you're serious."

I stepped on the gas, but the line up front didn't move. "They ain't budging," I yelled, and at the last minute I slammed on the brakes.

"Now you've done it. I thought you were white, but now I know you're yellow," Lester said, but he didn't have time to say anything else. A man jumped on the running board. Before either of us could say a word, an arm had reached in to grab Lester.

"Out of there, nigger!" the man yelled. "You got no call to be riding around with no white man." He yanked at Lester's arm. "Come on over here, boys. I found us a darky to hang, sure enough."

I was shocked because Lester didn't fight back. "Don't hurt me, boss," he said, and I almost passed out with surprise, but then suddenly I knew why he was acting so meek. The other men broke their roadblock formation and headed toward the truck. Just at that second, I gunned the gas pedal.

"Help," yelled the man on the running board. At first he was able to hold on, but I got up my speed and turned a corner fast. The man fell backward, taking the sleeve of Lester's blue chambray shirt with him.

"Damn cracker tore my shirt," Lester said.

"Reckon he'd done a sight worse than tear your shirt if I hadn't thought to speed up," I said, but if I expected any thanks from Lester, I sure didn't get any.

"I wasn't worried," he said. "I figured even a fool like you would see what to do if I bought you some time."

The preacher had last seen Isaac down in front of the courthouse, where all the trouble started. He was able to give me directions: After you get into town, just keep going east till you see a big building.

Lester didn't make no comments, and he sure wasn't any help in finding downtown. Finally I found the right place and pulled the truck over to park. Right off, I saw a man with a gun, keeping guard. "Get down," I told Lester, and he did. I jumped out of the truck. "I'm looking for my pa," I said to the man. "They told me he got hurt down here." I walked over to where he was standing, but all the time my eyes were darting around looking for Isaac.

"Ain't no injured whites left down here," he said. "Likely he's been took to the hospital already."

Just then I saw him. Isaac was laying between two other men. One of the men rolled over, and I got a view of Isaac in his new blue shirt. His eyes were closed, and he did not move. "Isaac," I yelled, and I ran to him.

The guard was right behind me. "You know this fellow?" he asked.

"Yes," I said. "He was my neighbor out in Wekiwa!" I dropped beside Isaac and put my hand on his heart. I could feel him breathing, but the movement of his chest didn't seem very strong to me. "Isaac," I said. "Open your eyes. It's me, Nobe. Please, Isaac." I started to cry.

The guard took my arm and jerked on it hard until I stood up. "Look, here, kid," he said. "You ain't supposed to be down here a'tall. What are you doing crying over some darky?"

"I want to take him to a doctor," I said. "You got to let me take him to a doctor."

I knew right off that I had used the wrong word. He gave me a shove. "I don't got to do anything except die some day. Now, sonny, if it is that you ain't exactly ready to die, I suggest you hightail it out of here."

"But he's hurt," I pleaded. "So are these other men."

"A truck will come and take them to be seen about," said the man.

"When?" I asked. "It's been hours since he was hurt."

My answer was a rifle in my ribs. "I said go. Now you best go."

Just then I heard Lester's yell. "Eenie meenie miney moe, catch a stupid whitey by the toe." It took me a second to spot him over by an alley.

"Halt and surrender," yelled the guard.

"Make me, fatso. You couldn't move your white rear fast enough to catch a turtle." He took off down the alley, and the guard headed after him. I knew I had to get Isaac in the truck, and I knew it had to be fast. I was running for the blanket when I heard two shots from the direction of the alley.

Lester? I wanted to yell out, but I knew it wouldn't do any good. I knew I had to move fast. If Lester caught them shots, he did it to save Isaac. I couldn't be the one to mess up. I grabbed the blanket and ran back to spread it at Isaac's head.

"Can you get me a drink, boy?" It was the man beside Isaac. He had opened his eyes, and they pleaded with me.

"I can't," I told him, and I pulled hard on Isaac. "I've got to hurry before the guard comes back." I had Isaac on the blanket then. I rolled him up in it and started to pull with all my might. "Isaac," I said, "I'm sorry about the bumps." There was no sound from him. When I was a few feet away, I thought about the man who was thirsty. "I'm sorry about the water," I called. He didn't answer either.

What happened next was the biggest surprise of the night. I was at the back of the truck, trying to lift Isaac up, when a dark shadow popped up from behind the truck. I almost screamed. "Lester," I said when I could talk, "how in the world did you get here?"

He laughed. "Climbed a building and ran across a few roofs. It doesn't take much to outwit some stupid cracker, thinks he's smart because he has a gun." When we got Isaac settled in the back, Lester climbed up beside him. "I'll ride back here with him," he said. "You get up front, get this thing moving, and don't you slow down till we get to Wekiwa."

"Don't you reckon we ought to take him to a doctor here somewhere?"

"No, not in this town, not tonight. Too dangerous."

I started to get in the truck, but instead I grabbed the jug of water and ran toward the thirsty man.

"What the devil are you doing?" Lester shouted, but I didn't take time to answer.

I dropped down, pulled the man's head up, and held the jug up to his lips. He got a big long drink. "I've got to run," I told him, and I did, with the jug in my hands.

"Give me that jug, you little fool," Lester said when I was back at the truck. Then I jumped inside and started it up.

Just before I started it up, I heard Lester shout, "If anyone stops us, I'll be stretched out beside Isaac. You just claim you've got two dead niggers."

I started wondering if maybe Lester was telling how it would be. Maybe they would both be dead and me too before the light of day would come to Tulsa, Oklahoma. I saw some awful things that night. It was strange knowing folks was dying right around me. There was fires everywhere, and it was like you could smell death in the smoke. It all seemed like some awful dream.

At one corner, I slowed down and saw a black man on his knees with three white guys standing over him with guns. The night air carried his words to me, and I wished I had never heard them. "Don't kill me," he pleaded. "I wasn't anyplace around that courthouse. Please, I got a wife and five children depending on me."

I wanted to cry out, but I didn't. I just gave that truck the gas and went on by. My tires had barely rolled over when I heard three shots. All three of them white guys had shot at once. I wanted to stop and vomit, but I didn't, just fought the sickness down. I thought about Preacher Jackson. No wonder he was so shook up. He's shell-shocked, I thought, just like poor Olly.

We was almost out of town when I saw a wooden roadblock up in front of me, and I had to slow down. I glanced back to see Lester lay down on his back beside Isaac. I had to smile just a little when I saw Lester cross his hands over his heart. I'll bet you ain't never looked that peaceful in your whole life before, Mr. Lester Cotton, I thought.

I didn't have time to enjoy the thought long. A soldier stuck a lantern in my face, and another one flashed one across the back of the truck, and yelled, "Two coloreds back here. Look dead."

"What you doing with dead coloreds in the back of your truck, son?" said the soldier.

I swallowed hard, trying to think what to say. "They ain't mine," I said, sort of stuttering. "A-aa soldier f-fellow, he stopped me and told me to take them to the edge of town. Said there'd be fellows there to get rid of them. I didn't k-kill n-nobody." I acted like I was about to cry.

The soldier reached in and sort of slapped my back. "Well, now, I never thought you did nothing wrong, but son, you got to toughen up. This here life ain't always pretty." He stepped down from my running board, and waved me on. "You're doing right," he yelled.

"I sure am," I said to myself. "I most surely am doing the rightest thing I ever done in my life."

When we was finally out of town, I pulled over, stuck my head out, and yelled. "How is he?"

"Still breathing," yelled Lester, "but just barely. The doctor at Wekiwa? Will he treat Isaac?"

For just a second I didn't know what Lester meant, but then I realized he wanted to know if Doc Sage would treat colored folks. "Sure he will," I yelled. "He's a good man."

"Then step on that pedal," he yelled, "and don't stop again until you're at the doc's place." I did. I made that old truck of the preacher's go as fast as it could go. We bounced down the road at an amazing speed. I worried about giving Isaac such a rough ride, but I figured rough was better than dead.

Chapter 7

MOST OF WEKIWA was dark when we drove in, but at the sheriff's house, a light was shining up in Ma's room. I knew Ma was walking that floor, wondering where I was and worrying about me. I felt bad about that, but it couldn't be helped. If I had told her where I was going, she'd have tried to stop me. I drove on by the house and turned down the next street to get to Doc Sage's place.

The doctor always had a light on in his front room because he expected visitors in the middle of the night. "Let me see if he's here," I told Lester when I jumped out. "He could be birthing a baby or something."

He was home, and he helped us get Isaac inside. We put him on the doctor's big examining table, and Doc turned on a big electric light above the table. We helped him take off Isaac's clothes, so he could look at every part of his body. The room was quiet. Lester walked off to stand by the window, like he wasn't really part of what went on. I stayed near the table, watching everything the doctor did.

Finally, Doc looked up at me. "No other marks," he said. "It's the bump on the head that's causing the trauma. How long has he been like this?"

Lester had turned back toward us, and Doc looked at Lester when he asked the question. Lester just shrugged his shoulders. I spoke up. "The preacher saw him get hit with a gun hours and hours ago."

"Here in Wekiwa?"

"Over in Tulsa. They've got bad trouble there between the whites and the coloreds. Isaac was just trying to stop it." I said.

"Isn't this Mrs. Mitchell's son?" Doc asked.

I looked at Lester, thinking he might say he was the father, but he just kept quiet. "Yes," I said.

"Take him to his mother," the doctor said. "I have a bed here in the house I could keep him in, but he'd be better off with her. Tell her she can squeeze a drop of water from a cloth into his mouth once in a while, but not to give him food or drink."

"Thanks, Doc," I said.

Lester surprised me by taking out his billfold. "How much?" he asked. It was the first time he had spoken.

"I won't charge Mrs. Mitchell's son," he said. "The woman is a saint on earth, teaches children all day after sitting up with the sick half the night. She's going to take this real hard, sets a lot of store in that boy, she does." I looked over at Lester and wondered how much store he set in Isaac.

The doctor helped us get Isaac back in the truck, and I fired it up before I thought about Ma. I got out and went to the back to explain to Lester that I had to stop at the sheriff's house. I took off my boots at the door, and I was real quiet going up the stairs on account of the sheriff and his wife and not wanting to deal with his attitude toward what I was doing. Ma was in her room.

"Praise God," Ma said when she saw me, and she come over to me and touched my face. I couldn't remember the last time Ma had touched me with warm feeling inside her, and I figured she must have been real worried about me.

"I had to go over to Tulsa," I said.

"Thanks to Daisy I happened to discover that." She was over her worrying now, and real riled. "When you didn't come home, I went over to see Daisy, and she told me you left with the cook." She pressed her lips together like she always did when she was about to bust with being mad. "Poor Daisy. She had so many dirty dishes stacked up, and her without no cook, either. I stayed and helped out some. A person would think you might consider your job even if you don't mind leaving your own mother worrying till she's half out of her mind."

"Ma," I said, "they had bad trouble over in Tulsa."

She folded her arms across her chest. "Wasn't your trouble to mix in. Sheriff Leonard told me that the coloreds were going wild."

"Seems to me it was the whites that went wild. Isaac Mitchell got hit in the head, and all he done was try to get people to calm down."

"Isaac Mitchell and his mother ain't yours to tend to."

"Ma," I said, real tired and low. "He might die."

She softened a little. "Now, I am right sorry to hear that. I wouldn't wish that kind of heartbreak on no mother."

"I got to go now, and take Isaac home."

I was almost to the door when Ma reached out her hand to grab my arm. "Be real quiet coming and going. I don't want Dudley to know you was mixing in with the coloreds. He don't see things like you do, and we got to live here."

I looked at her for a minute before I answered. I thought about the fire and the awful smoke. I remembered the man on his knees begging for his life. I knew I wasn't never going to be the same after what I had just seen.

"Yes, Ma," I said, " I'll be quiet. I know how the sheriff sees things, and I know we got to live here." I started out the door, and then I turned back. "But I'll tell you one thing more. I'm glad you've decided to help Mrs. Leonard, but still, I ain't living here long. I done promised myself that." I closed the door behind me and tiptoed down the stairs.

On the second floor, I could hear Sheriff Leonard snoring. I stopped and listened for just a minute, hating him. It was different than yesterday. I thought about how I couldn't turn loose of the hating even if I had wanted to, but it sort of scared me too, thinking how hating was what caused all that burning over in Tulsa. It started to turn around in my head that hate was a killer, even when the person doing the hating was on the right side.

Mrs. Mitchell's house was dark. She was in there, sleeping peaceful and not knowing what awful thing had happened. I was glad Lester was with me. He could go knock on the door and tell her, but that's not how he had made it up in his mind to happen.

I got out and went back to them. Lester was getting out too, but he turned to me. "Go wake her up," he said.

"Me?"

"She'd rather hear it from you than from me. Besides, I don't know as she knows I am in these parts. The shock of seeing me would just confuse the news about Isaac. You tell her I'm out here before she sees me." I didn't move, and he gave me a little shove. "I said go."

If he'd done that any other time, I'd have laid into him. "You ain't any better than Sheriff Leonard or them white people that hurt Isaac," I said, "you're all just alike." With a sad heart, I went up to pound on the back door. I saw a lantern light come on in the house.

"I'm coming," she called.

I knew she'd figure it was some colored person with a sick one at home, asking for her help. I stepped up close to an open window and said real loud, "It's me, Nobe. I got to talk to you."

I should of told her then, I said to myself, got it over with before she come to the door, before I had to look in her face.

"Let me throw on a dress," she said, and she didn't even sound rattled. She was used to trouble in the night, but the trouble usually belonged to some other poor soul. This trouble would be staying right here in Mrs. Mitchell's own little house, right along with all the flower beds and window boxes.

When she opened the door, I didn't try to break it easy, just blurted out, "It's Isaac. He got hurt over in Tulsa."

She didn't scream, just sucked in her breath real hard. "How? How's he hurt?" She leaned out around me, trying to see what I come in.

"He got hit in the head, real hard. He ain't awake. The doc says it's a concussion of the brain."

"He's unconscious? Oh, no! Where is he?"

"He's out in the truck. Doc said he might as well be here with you." She started to step around me, going to the truck.

"Wait a second, ma'am. I got something else to tell you. Isaac's pa, he's out there too. He wanted me to tell you."

She made that surprised sound with her breath again, but she went right on out to the back of the truck.

"Martha," Lester said when we got to the back.

"Don't talk to me, Lester Cotton," she said. "You don't come around your son for years and years, and when you do, you get him hurt."

I thought Lester would explode into how he didn't get Isaac hurt, but he didn't. He didn't say nothing to defend himself, just said, "Let's get him into the house." He did something then that surprised me. He lifted Isaac up in his own arms.

I didn't see how he could do that, being pretty scrawny and all. "Let me help you," I said, but he shook his head.

"I can carry my boy," he said.

Mrs. Mitchell ran ahead and pulled back the cover on the bed in Isaac's little room. I had been in that room before, but it looked different now, sort of lonely. It had nice flowered wallpaper. There was a desk with some books on it, and on the wall was a picture of an important-looking colored man in a suit. I never had asked who he was.

After Lester laid Isaac down, he turned and walked out of the house. Didn't say a word to Mrs. Mitchell or to me. I stayed while Mrs. Mitchell washed Isaac's face, and I told her what the doctor had said about the drops of water. Then I told her that if there wasn't anything I could do to help, I'd be going on my way.

On the way out, I thought about explaining that Lester didn't get Isaac into trouble. I stopped at the door and opened my mouth, but I didn't know how to say what I wanted to say. Instead I said, "Who's that in the picture?"

"Booker T. Washington," she said, but she didn't look up, just kept wiping at Isaac's face. "He was an educator and a leader of our people." Her voice got real sad, and she said, "Isaac always looked up to him."

Truth be told, I wasn't much interested right then in Mr. Booker T. Washington, but I was stalling for time. "Is he dead now?" I asked.

"Yes, Booker T. Washington is dead," she said, and she sort of moaned.

"There's something else, Mrs. Mitchell, ma'am, something else I got to say to you."

She looked up at me then. "Say it, Noble."

I took a deep breath and started. "Well, Lester, he didn't get Isaac into any trouble. There was terrible trouble between colored people and white people in Tulsa. Preacher Jackson saw it all start. He saw Isaac get hurt, but he didn't see him after. The preacher come into Daisy's and told us about it. I borrowed his truck, and Lester went along to help. He sure was a help, got a guard to chase him so I could take Isaac to the truck. He took lots of chances, him being colored and all. He could have got killed. There was a lot of colored folks killed and the whole colored section burned."

She nodded her head. "I was wrong," she said, "and I will apologize to Mr. Cotton. However, you shouldn't trouble yourself over his being unjustly accused. Mr. Lester Cotton is far from an innocent man in the great scheme of things."

"Yes, ma'am," I said, and I went on out. When the lights from the truck hit the side of the house, I saw Lester. He had taken a chair from Mrs. Mitchell's front porch. He was setting in it, leaned back against the wall, right under Isaac's window. I figured he'd set there until daylight, and I wondered if he'd sing.

On the trip back to the sheriff's, I kept thinking about how Isaac and me met up the first time. It was before I started selling milk to Mrs. Mitchell. I was pretty little, maybe eight or nine, and Pa had just given me a licking with his belt. I had places on my back that were still bleeding and stinging something awful.

I went down to the creek, took off my overalls, and got in the water, even though it was just spring, and the water was still cold. I had climbed out and put back on my overalls. I was setting on a rock in the sun, trying to make my teeth quit chattering, when Isaac showed up.

He had walked up behind me without me knowing it until he said, "Hello." I whirled around to look at him, standing there with a fishing pole in his hand and a big smile on his face.

I must have kind of jumped when he spoke to me, because he said, "Don't be afraid. I won't eat you or anything."

"I ain't scared," I said, sort of tough like. "I ain't scared of nothing."

"Wow," said Isaac, "is that right? You're a lot braver than I am. I'm scared of lots of things." He laid his pole on the grass and set right down on the big rock beside me.

Isaac had just finished high school, and he was fixing to go to college somewhere off in another state, but he told me that his mother had just moved in down the road to be the new teacher at the colored school, and that he was spending some time with her.

Isaac made me laugh with a funny story about a bear named Fuzzy Wass He, and then he asked me what happened to my back.

At first I didn't want to tell him, but he had such a kind face. "My pa used a belt to give me a licking," I said.

A sort of angry look came to Isaac's face, and he said, "He shouldn't be allowed to do that."

I shrugged. "I reckon pas can do whatever they've a mind to with their own young'uns."

"I'm afraid you're right," he said, "but it shouldn't be that way. What does your mother say when he beats you?"

"Ma don't say much to hinder what Pa sets his mind to," I said.

Isaac just shook his head. "Say," he said, "is this a good fishing place?"

"Never tried it," I said. "Don't know how to fish."

"Well," said Isaac, "it's time you learned."

We fished all afternoon. Mostly I held the pole, with Isaac giving me instructions. We caught three good-size fish and one little one.

"We'll put this little guy back," Isaac said. "Let him grow."

It come to me just at that minute, watching Isaac slip that fish off the hook, that here was a fellow that would always be kind to little critters and little people. He had the kindest big brown eyes that I had ever seen. I knew Pa always said you couldn't trust a colored person, and Isaac was the first one I'd ever talked to. I was old enough, though, to know that Pa was wrong about lots of things.

Isaac gave me the fish we caught, and he gave me the fishing pole. I was real proud to take the fish home for Ma to cook. I told Ma and Pa that I had met a fellow at the creek who helped me catch the fish, but I didn't tell them the fellow was colored.

All that spring, I'd slip out and meet Isaac at the creek for fishing. Sometimes we'd go to his house. He taught me how to play baseball and marbles. I got so good at marbles that I could beat him fair and square. Isaac would always laugh when I beat him and say, "I taught you too well."

After Isaac taught me to play, I won lots of marbles from the boys at school. I liked to look at them because they reminded me of Isaac.

Before too long, Isaac had to leave for college. I walked out to the main road with him to wait for the bus. "Why do colored folks always set in the back of the bus?" I asked him.

"Because that's the law the white men made. It isn't right, but it will change some day." He reached down and put his hand on my head. "Lots of things in life aren't right, Nobe, but most things get better with time."

I remember that when Isaac got on that bus, I felt so lonesome, lots more lonesome than I had ever felt before. I stood and waved at the bus until it disappeared in the dust.

That's how I got to know Mrs. Mitchell, by going over there with Isaac to eat. She started right from the beginning to call me Noble instead of Nobe.

Ma found out somehow about me spending so much time with Isaac and his mother. She didn't like it much, but she didn't tell Pa. Ma never did anything to stop Pa when he beat me, but she'd spare me if she could. Sometimes after I got back from eating with the Mitchells, Ma would ask me what we had. She'd want to know too what kind of dishes we used, what the furniture looked like, and how things was arranged.

Ma was real interested when I talked about things like Mrs. Mitchell's flowers or the nice starched tablecloth on the table. She never had heard of colored folks having nice things. She didn't think it was right, but she wanted to hear about it anyway.

I stopped the truck in front of the drive to our old place. No one had moved in there yet, so I drove up in front of the old house. The moon was big and round in the sky, and it put a sort of soft light all over. Things looked pretty good in that light. I knowed if I looked real close all around that I would see that little fellow, the one with yellow hair and quick blue eyes that were always on the lookout to see if he could keep from getting hit.

I knew I could see Pa out there beside the barn too, but I didn't look. I just set there in that truck, and I prayed. "God," I said, "don't let Isaac die. I reckon he's the truest kind of Christian there is. If you let him die, don't expect to be hearing from me again, because I just won't have no use for you if you let that happen." Then I thought to say, "In the name of Jesus," like the preacher does in church, before I said, "amen." I felt real glad about adding that part about in the name of Jesus, because from what I heard about Jesus, I figured Isaac was more like him than any other man I had ever met.

Chapter 8

I SLEPT LATE the next morning. When I started down the stairs, I could hear Ma and Mrs. Leonard on the second floor. Ma was helping Mrs. Leonard practice her walking, and I stopped to see if they needed a hand.

They were outside the bedroom door, Mrs. Leonard close to the wall and holding tight to Ma. "You're doing so good, Mavis," Ma said. Then she looked up to see me. "Oh, Nobe, there you are. I saved some breakfast for you on the back of the stove."

Mrs. Leonard leaned against the wall and looked at me. "Mercy," she said, "when I look at you, I almost call you Joe."

"I hope seeing me don't make you sad," I said.

"Mercy, no." She smiled. "It's a blessing, a pure blessing, to lay eyes on you."

"Ma," I said, "I aim to go out to the Mitchells' after I'm finished working. I sure am anxious to hear about Isaac."

Mrs. Leonard was moving again, and Ma held tight to her arm. "I was just telling Mavis about you driving to Tulsa last night to help that boy." She smiled at me, kind of embarassed, like she wanted me to know she was sorry for fussing at me. "Mavis thinks it was a real brave thing for you to do."

"I do," said Mrs. Leonard. She let go of Ma's arm and reached out to take mine. "What's right is right, and I told your mother she ought to be real proud of you for seeing what had to be done."

"Thank you, ma'am," I said, and I helped Ma get her back to bed.

"You're a deal stronger than you was at first," Ma told her while she fluffed up the pillow. Just then we heard the sheriff on the stairs.

"Vivian," he shouted. "Where's that boy of yours?"

"We're all in here," Mavis called.

The sheriff's big form filled the doorway. His face was red, and I knew he was mad. "I've got plans for you today," he said. "You can whitewash the fence, keep you out of trouble."

"I got to be at the café before long," I said. "I'll do the fence tomorrow."

"You'll do it when you get off." The sheriff folded his arms across his chest and glared at me.

"Dudley," said Mrs. Leonard, "the fence can wait. I'm sending Nobe on an errand for me after he gets off work." Ma's hand was still on the pillow. I saw Mrs. Leonard reach over and give Ma's hand a quick squeeze.

I stood real still, wondering what would happen when the sheriff demanded to know what errand I was going to do, but he didn't ask, just let his breath out in a sort of sigh.

"Well, tomorrow, then. I don't want you with time on your hands and hanging out with coloreds."

"Dudley, I wish you wouldn't be so pigheaded," said his

wife. "But you don't have to worry about this boy. He knows what's right."

The sheriff looked at her real close, like he was trying to figure out if she was making fun of him. I stared down at the floor, so as I wouldn't grin.

"Nobe," Ma said, "you ought to go down and eat your breakfast."

I was glad to have a reason to get away from the sheriff. I slid past him and down the stairs, but I heard his heavy steps behind me. I got the plate from the back of the stove where Ma had put it to keep the biscuits and gravy warm.

The sheriff came into the kitchen and poured a cup of coffee from the pot on the stove, then settled at the little kitchen table.

"Sheriff," I said, real sweet like, "ain't it likely the whole town is running amok without you to watch it?"

"Don't get smart with me, boy. Set yourself down here to eat," the sheriff said. "I come home special to talk to you."

I lost my appetite when he said that, but I did like he said. I took a bite while I waited for him to talk. "I want to know what's going on with that colored kid," he said.

"Isaac Mitchell?"

He grunted and nodded his head. "Heard you went up to Tulsa to bring him home last night."

It was my turn to nod.

"Well," he said. "What's going on?"

"Isaac's hurt. He's unconscious, or at least he was last night. He's at his mother's. That's all I know."

He grunted again, and he stood up. "You see here, I won't put up with no trouble out of the coloreds in this town. You might just pass that on to your darky friends!"

"I don't think Isaac's got starting any trouble on his mind. He sure didn't look like it last night, unconscious in his bed."

"You just pass on what I said. Hear?" He stood up.

I nodded and bolted away from the table and through the back door. "Nobe," my mother yelled out from upstairs, "you didn't eat your breakfast." I didn't look back in her direction.

It was too early for me to go to work, but I went on over to the café anyway. I was mostly hoping Lester would be there and that I could find out about Isaac.

Lester wasn't there. "He comes in at eleven today," Daisy told me. She had lots of questions about the Tulsa trip, but I gave her pretty short answers. I guess I just wasn't much interested in a discussion, and I sure didn't want to let on about Lester being Isaac's pa. I went on back in the kitchen

Lida Rose was in there, and she had on a new red dress. She jumped up from her chair so I could see it well. "Mama ordered it for me from the Sears catalog," she said, "but they've got a little red hat that would just go with it over in Hill's window. Ain't that lucky? Mama might buy the hat for me too."

"You look mighty pretty," I told her, and she did. She was the prettiest little girl I'd ever seen in that new red dress! She went back to playing with paper dolls.

"This is the little girl," she said, holding up a small doll. "She is an only child like me, but she hopes her mama and daddy will get her a baby brother or sister for a surprise."

"What's her name?" I asked.

"Oh, her name is Dottie Dimple. See, this is her friend, Lottie Love." She held up another doll.

"That's nice," I said, and I went to sit at the little table in the corner.

Lida Rose brought her dolls over to the table and spread them out. "Do you have a sister, Nobe?" she asked.

"No sisters. No brothers," I said.

"Me either," she said. "I wish I did have a brother." She leaned close to me. "He would play with me." Her pigtails bounced when she moved her head, and she studied me real close with her big blue eyes. "Well," she said. "You could be sort of my pretend brother."

"What does a pretend brother do?" I asked.

She sighed, like I was sure a trial to her patience. "The same thing a real brother does, of course. He plays with me."

I didn't feel like playing, but she smiled so sweet, I just nodded. "I'll play if I don't have to move none," I said. "I'm pretty tuckered out this morning."

That sounded fine to Lida Rose. "You just set right there," she said. "I'll be Zorro and do all the moving."

"Zero?" I said. I knew better, but I wanted to razz Lida Rose just a little.

"Not Zero!" She rolled her eyes. "Zero is nothing. Seems like a big boy like you would know that." I opened my mouth to defend myself, say I did know about zeroes, but she didn't give me a chance. "Zorro! He's this guy in the picture show. He lives where there are lots of bad guys."

"Tulsa?" I said. This time I wasn't trying to tease. I was just remembering the awful burning. "Or maybe right here in Wekiwa. We've got us one or two of those bad guys."

"No," she said, trying to be patient. "It's some place far away."

"Like California, maybe." I had never seen Zorro because there wasn't no picture show in Wekiwa, but I had heard about him. "Zorro is this Mexican guy who wears a mask and goes around helping out poor people who are in trouble."

Lida Rose clapped her hands. "You do know Zorro. Good. Well, I'm Zorro, and you are the bad guy."

"Do I have a name?"

"We'll just call you the bad guy."

"Okay," I used my finger as a gun. "I've just shot at some poor people."

Lida Rose threw up her hand. "Wait! What will we do about my friend. Zorro has to have a friend?" She frowned. "We need one other person to be my friend." She looked around the room and grabbed a broom. "This will have to be him."

Just then Lester came through the back door. "Gosh," said Lida Rose, pointing at him with her head. "He could be the bad guy, and you could be my friend." She lowered her voice just a little. "He'd make a good bad guy." She studied Lester's face and shook her head. "I'm pretty positive there ain't no use to ask him does he want to play."

"I suspect you're right," I said, "but I've got to talk to Mr. Cotton before we start our game."

Lida Rose gave a little impatient sigh, but she let me talk. "How's Isaac?" I asked.

For a second, Lester looked at me like he wasn't going to answer, but he did. "Reckon you could go out there and ask him yourself."

I jumped up. "He's awake?"

"Wasn't talking when we hauled him in there last night, was he?"

I grabbed Lida Rose's hands and started to do a little dance with her. "When did he wake up?" I asked.

"You want to know every little detail, you've got to go out

there." He turned to take his apron from the hook. "They don't pay me to stand around jawing all day."

"What's he talking about?" Lida Rose asked.

I just smiled. "He's trying to play like he's a bad man," I told her, "but the thing is, I know better."

"Are you here to flap your gums or to wash dishes?" Lester pointed at a stack of dishes beside the sink.

"I am here to play," I said, and I laughed. "Yes, sir, that's my true purpose." I moved my chair over to the corner, and for thirty minutes I was the bad guy while Lida Rose and her buddy the broom went around rescuing folks from the terrible things I done. She laughed a bunch too, and I couldn't stop smiling.

When the noon crowd came in to eat, I had to quit playing and tackle the dishes, but I still felt good, like a little kid who just got a full sack of candy. As soon as my work time was up, I headed out to Mrs. Mitchell's place.

I reckon I never did enjoy a walk more than I did that one, me with my heart all light, and that whole June day just as sweet as the little roses that were growing wild on some of the fences I passed. The first two miles I just enjoyed the day, and once I called out to a cow, "Hey there, old girl, Isaac is awake. I reckon the world ain't too bad a place, after all."

In the last mile there was three important places. Before I got to Cinda's, my mind got off Isaac and how glad I was to know he was all right. I went to thinking about Cinda. I didn't have no impure thoughts though. I just thought how she was like a sunflower, fresh and strong. I hoped maybe she'd be in the yard, swinging on that same swing where I'd seen her the first time or hoeing in the garden, but there wasn't no sight of her.

I wanted to stop and knock on her door. I thought about how Basil Bailey and his plane would likely be landing over at

Widow Carter's place any minute now. I'd heard Basil and Willie was coming to stay with Olly the night before. Some folks was talking about going out to the widow's to watch them land.

Tomorrow was June 2, and I would get paid in the morning. Me and Cinda would be going on another plane ride in the afternoon. I didn't stop, though. I turned sort of shy. Cinda might ask why I stopped. I'd already told her to meet me at the widow's place tomorrow. Besides, I was in sort of a hurry to see Isaac. I just walked on by her house, but just in case, I looked back over my shoulder every once in a while until I couldn't see her house.

After Cinda's, it wasn't long until our old home place was in view. I didn't look over that way, not once, and I started to whistle. I didn't want to see Pa or me, the little boy with the lonely look on his face. I couldn't stand to look at that little boy, not on a day when my heart was so filled up with springtime and gladness. I just kept my head turned, and I kept right on whistling.

It wasn't long before I saw Mrs. Mitchell's place. When I got close enough to see the flowers in the window box, I couldn't walk anymore. I broke into a run, and I had to hold myself back from yelling out to Isaac and his mother.

Even outside I could smell the beans and cornbread. I'd had me a bite to eat at the café, but I knew I'd eat again if I was asked, and I knew I'd be asked. Mrs. Mitchell came to the door when I knocked. "Come in, come in," she said. "Isaac's up." She grabbed my hand and pulled me inside.

He was setting at the table, but he got up when I walked in. "There's my rescuer," he said, and he punched me on the shoulder like he always does.

"I had help," I said, and I looked over at Mrs. Mitchell and wondered what she'd said to Isaac about the night before.

"Old Lester," he said, and he shook his head in wonder. "Mama told me you said he risked his life."

"He did," I said. "He got two guards to chase him, and he climbed over a building. I couldn't of done it without him."

"Sit down." Mrs. Mitchell pulled out a chair for me. "Cornbread's ready to come out of the oven, and I'd like nothing better than having my two favorite young men at my table."

I did, and boy was I hungry. The beans had big pieces of juicy ham in them, and I never tasted cornbread so sweet and good. After we finished, we just stayed at the table talking and laughing, mostly about airplanes and my experience with Basil Bailey. Isaac was interested in going up when Basil came to town the next day.

I figured Isaac wanted to talk more about the riot and about Lester, but he didn't want to talk in front of his mother. I wasn't surprised when after I said I had to go, Isaac said, "How about I use your car, Mama, to drive Nobe back to town?"

"You know that automobile is yours to use any time. After all, you did buy it. But are you sure you're up to driving?" She leaned across the table to look at him carefully.

He waved his hand toward his empty plate. "Don't you suppose it would take a pretty healthy fellow to put away that amount of beans and cornbread?"

Mrs. Mitchell smiled. Then her face got real serious. "You aren't planning to go back to Tulsa tonight, are you? I want you to stay away from there for a while."

"No." Isaac let his breath go in a sad sigh. "There's no rush for me to go back. There's no job to go back to, not even any bank building." He held his hands out in front of him and studied them like words were written there. "I still can't be-lieve it."

Mrs. Mitchell got up and moved to put her hand on his shoulder. "You're alive. My boy's alive." Her voice broke. "It could have been the other way."

Isaac patted her hand, and then he stood up. "Well, Mr. Nobe," he said. "I'm ready when you are."

He didn't mention me driving. I wanted to, but I didn't say nothing. Later I thought about that a bunch. It could have been me that was behind the wheel when we drove into Wekiwa.

We had just barely turned away from the house to the main road when Isaac asked, "See him today, did you?"

I knew he was talking about Lester. "Yeah," I said. "He told me you were awake."

"He stayed outside my window all night." His voice had a strange, sort of faraway sound to it. "I heard him singing when I was unconscious. I know I did, and he was still out there when I woke up."

He stopped talking, but I didn't say nothing because I knew it wasn't that kind of stop. He had more to say and was just get-ting ready because he was fixing to say something big. When he went on, his voice sounded even stranger. "The funny thing is the song he was singing while I was out. I remember it now. He used to sing it to me all the time when I was little. See, I never remembered anything about him before, never anything about the time before they split up. I never remembered hav-ing a father at all, but I did. I had a father, and he sang to me."

"I'm glad," I said. "It's a nice thing to remember, having your pa sing you a lullaby." I looked out the window just then without realizing I'd see our place, but there it was. Sure enough I saw him. Pa was standing by the barn, sort of lean-ing against it. He had on that old straw hat that Ma put in the box with him. I didn't see that little blond boy, but something funny happened. Just before I lost sight of the ghost, he looked up and saw me, and he took off that hat and waved it. I wished that we'd been closer to the barn on account of I wondered if the ghost was smiling at me. I really, really won-dered that.

"I want to see him again," Isaac said. "Do you know where he stays at night?"

I told him that I didn't. "He's at the café sometimes around suppertime. Sometimes Daisy does the evening cook-ing herself, but sometimes Lester comes in for it."

He didn't say anything for about a half a mile. We just rode along in silence, Isaac thinking about his pa and me about mine. Then Isaac said, "Will you tell him I want to see him and ask him to tell you when and where?" He sort of bit at his lip. "I can't ask him myself. Doesn't that sound silly, me being a grown man and all? But I just can't."

"No, it don't sound silly," I said, "not to a fellow like me. I reckon I been there, same as you. The difference being that you still got a chance to get that blessing, the one pas give their sons."

We rode along without talking for a while, then I said, "Isaac, what are you going to do about them white folks? You know, the ones that went crazy and burned up Black Wall Street."

"Do about them?"

"Well, the law sure wasn't acting like they was going to put them in jail or anything. Leastways, I didn't see no sign of it the other night. Seems like it was the coloreds got all the blame."

"Yes," Isaac said. "We weren't blameless, not in the beginning. There shouldn't have been a mob of us down there. The law was not going to let anyone get lynched, but there's no excuse for what Mama told me you saw happen later, all those innocent people getting their homes and businesses burned. I wonder if anyone even knows how many innocent people died, all because hate got out of hand."

"So, if the law ain't going to do anything, what are you going to do?"

Isaac shook his head, and he smiled a sort of sad little smile. "Maybe I won't ever go back to Tulsa." He sort of bit at his lip. "Nothing to go back to really." He shrugged. "But maybe I will. Maybe I can find some kind of work there, and just maybe there'll be folks who can start to rebuild. If there are any, maybe I'll help out some. Guess I'll wait and see what happens."

I could see he hadn't understood my question, so I tried again. "But what about getting even? If the law ain't going to do something, shouldn't you? Shouldn't you do something to sort of get those bad guys that picked on them innocent people and burned their places and all? Shouldn't you do something like that guy Zorro does in the picture shows?"

Isaac smiled. "I think Zorro is Mexican, not colored," he said. "No, Nobe, I won't try to get even. There's just no profit in it. Getting even just generates more hate, and hate multiplies. It has a way of turning back on those who do the hating and eating them away."

"But you'd be right," I said. "You'd be right to get even."

Isaac shook his head. "A very wise person once told me that it is better to do right than to be right. If I do right, I'll try to make peace with white people."

"Who?" I asked. "Who told you that?"

"My mother," he said. "Martha Mitchell. The same woman who always calls you Noble instead of Nobe."

"Well, maybe she knows all about doing right, but she sure don't know much about me. I'm Nobe. There ain't one little part of me that's Noble. When somebody hurts me or my dog, I get even."

"No." Isaac shook his head. "I'm not interested in getting even, but I'll tell you something, Nobe. I'm beginning to think maybe that Professor Du Bois might have been partly right. Maybe it is time for colored people to start to stand up for ourselves, speak out for what's right."

I wanted to ask how Isaac thought he'd go about that, but I never got to ask because of what happened next. We was in town by then, just rounding the corner on Main Street. Isaac had just finished saying that about changing his mind when suddenly there was something moving, running right into the street. At first I only saw a red blur, but then in a split second I knew. Lida Rose! Lida Rose in her new red dress.

"God, no!" Isaac yelled, and he slammed on the brakes.

We couldn't stop in time. I felt a horrible bump. That's when I heard a scream, and I kept hearing it over and over. The car swerved. Isaac grabbed hard at the wheel, and he brought the car to a stop. My head bounced back and forth, and I sort of lost track of what was happening. I didn't lose track of that screaming, though. The screaming filled up the whole car, and even before I had a chance to look out of the window, I knew it was Daisy making that terrible sound.

Chapter 9

WE JUMPED OUT of the car to see people gathering around something in the street. I couldn't see very well, but I saw something red. "Get the doc," someone shouted.

"Isaac," I yelled, "we hit her!"

He came around from his side of the car. "I know," he said. "She ran right out in front of me, and I hit her. I hit that little girl." He leaned against the car.

For just a second, I was confused, unable to move, but then I pushed my way through the people. Daisy was on the ground, holding Lida Rose's head. Daisy had stopped screaming. Her face looked like it had been painted white, and her eyes stared out in front of her like they had been just painted on too and weren't real at all.

I dropped down beside them, and I took hold of Lida Rose's hand. "Lida Rose," I said. Then I turned to Daisy. "Can she talk?" I asked, but Daisy didn't say anything.

I heard someone say, "Out of my way," and I knew Doc Sage was coming.

I moved so he could get to Lida Rose. He knelt down, took her arm, lifted her eyelid, and put his hand on her chest. "This child is dead," he said.

There were sounds of disbelief and sorrow from the crowd. Daisy started to moan and to rock back and forth. I tried to lift my foot to go to her, but I couldn't. My whole body felt too heavy to move, like it was made of cement.

A woman from the crowd came to pull Daisy up and away from the body. Doc Sage lifted Lida Rose up in his arms. The crowd parted, and Doc walked with Lida Rose toward the furniture store. The belt of her new red dress trailed after them.

Then I remembered Isaac, and the heaviness left me. I whirled around to see the car. Isaac still stood there beside it, but he was not alone. Sheriff Leonard stood beside him, and Isaac had on handcuffs.

"Oh, no," I yelled, and I ran to stand beside Isaac. "You can't arrest Isaac," I said. "It was an accident. Just a terrible accident. Lida Rose run right out in front of us. There wasn't a thing Isaac could do about it."

Sheriff Leonard gave me a disgusted look. "Who pulled your chain?" he asked. "I don't recollect asking you what should I do."

"You can't arrest a man for hitting someone who run right out in front of him." My hands were clenched into fists, ready to fight.

"Look here." The sheriff pointed to his badge. "Do you see this here? Well, that badge means I am the law in this town. I decide who gets arrested. It ain't none of your call, but if you'll calm yourself down, I'll tell you I'm taking this boy in for his own protection." He pointed with his head toward the crowd of people still in the street. "That crowd's fixing to turn mean."

I looked at the people. Some were crying, some shaking their heads as they talked to each other. I didn't see anyone who seemed angry. Then I saw Cinda. There was people between us, but she was pushing her way through. I stood there waiting, and she never took her eyes off me as she moved.

"My father and I saw the accident, Sheriff," she called out when she got close. "Just ask him. He can tell you it wasn't Isaac's fault."

"Ain't no shortage of young ones in this town trying to do my job for me," he grumbled, and he gave Isaac a shove. "Move on to the jail, boy," he said.

Isaac started walking, but he turned his head toward me. "Let my mother know what happened," he said. "Take her car home and tell her."

"I will," I said. "I'll tell Lester too." I stood there watching until the sheriff and Isaac went inside the jail.

Cinda stood beside me, and she reached out to put her hand on my arm. That's how I learned that I was shaking. I saw Cinda's hand shaking with my arm. "Nobe," she said real soft. "Oh, Nobe."

I wanted to sit down and cry, but I didn't. "I got to get hold of myself," I said, and I started to walk. "I got to tell his mama." I swallowed hard. "And I've got to go tell his father."

"Father?" Cinda walked beside me. "I didn't know Isaac had a father."

"He works over at Daisy's." I kept walking. "I got to see him, but don't tell anyone he's Isaac's pa."

"That hateful colored man? He's Isaac's daddy?"

I just nodded. The front door of the café was standing open. I figured Daisy must have been standing in the door when she saw Lida Rose run out into the street. No one was in the front. No sound came from the back, but I went on through the swinging doors. Lester wasn't there, but there was an envelope on the table. It had my name on it, and under the name it said, "Give this to Isaac."

"It's a letter," I said to Cinda. "Lester left a letter here for Isaac. It must have been before. I guess Lester wasn't here, so he doesn't know." I stuck the letter in my overalls. "I'll give it to Isaac," I said, "but first I've got to tell his mama."

"I'm going with you," Cinda said. Then she stopped walking and looked down at the ground, kind of shy like. "I mean, if you want me to."

I just reached out and took her hand. We got in the car. At first we didn't talk much, but at the edge of town I started telling her about what happened in Tulsa. I talked about the burning, about the thirsty man, about how Lester saved Isaac and played dead, about the man who begged for his life and died anyway. I told it without no pauses, words just billowing out like the black smoke out of Tulsa. The last thing I said was, "We went through all that, and Isaac come out okay. Now God only knows what that devil sheriff is going to do to him right here in Wekiwa."

"Nothing bad's going to happen to him," Cinda said. "You'll think of something."

"Huh?" I said, and I shook my head. "Not me! Maybe his mama. Maybe Mrs. Mitchell can do something."

We was there then, stopping in front of that neat little house with the flowers in window boxes. I had to force my hand to reach for the door handle. I sure dreaded telling Mrs.

Mitchell what had happened. I kept hearing Doc Sage say, "She sets a lot of store by that boy."

The knock sounded loud in my ears, but I guess it really wasn't. I could hear Mrs. Mitchell's Victrola from the living room, and I knew I had to knock louder. When I did, she come to the door right off.

"Noble," she said, "and Cinda. How nice." She stepped aside. "Come in, please."

Cinda started to move, but I put out my hand to stop her. "We'll just wait here." I swallowed hard. "We brung your car. I reckon you'll want to go to town."

"My car?" She leaned out to look. "Where's Isaac?"

"That's the thing. See, there was an accident. We hit little Lida Rose Harrison." My voice broke then, and I looked over at Cinda. She knew I wanted her to finish.

"She's dead, ma'am," Cinda said real soft. "Everyone knows Isaac couldn't help it, but the sheriff took Isaac to jail. He claims it's just to make sure nobody hurts him."

Just like before, she didn't scream or cry, just sucked in her breath in that way she has with bad news. "I don't trust Sheriff Leonard," she said. "Why would he take Isaac to jail to protect him if there hadn't even been any talk about the accident being his fault?"

I agreed with her. "More likely he plans to stir up some trouble," I said.

"I've got to go to town," she said. "Let me get my purse."

The sheriff jumped up from his chair when we went into the jail. "Mrs. Mitchell, ma'am," he said. "I don't want you fretting over your boy. I'm just wanting to make sure no hotheads get stirred up over what happened."

Mrs. Mitchell didn't say much, and the sheriff let her in to see Isaac. Cinda and I waited out front. I spent my time looking at the folks as they walked up and down the sidewalk. I studied their faces, wondering if there really were people there who would hurt Isaac. I saw Daisy and Sim Harrison come out of Jones Furniture Store, and I knew they had been there to see about Lida Rose, about her box and burial.

I left Cinda and crossed the street. When I was in front of them, I went shy. There didn't seem to be nothing for me to say to them, but I tried. "I hate what happened," I said. "I hate it a powerful lot."

Then Daisy held out her arms. I went to her, and she held me close for a minute. "She loved you, Nobe," she said. "That little girl was just plumb crazy about you."

"I ain't never knowed any other little kids," I said. "I sure did like to watch her play." Then I thought of something else. "Isaac couldn't help what happened," I said.

"I know," Daisy said. "I saw her. She had gone over to look in the window of Hill's. There was a little hat there that she wanted to wear with her new red dress. We always told her not to cross the street, and she never had before. I was coming to take her across, but she'd already crossed. I think she was afraid I'd scold her, and she wanted to get back to the other side before I noticed. That's what she thought just before she died, that I would be mad at her." Daisy started to sob.

Sim put his arm around her. "I got to take her home," he said. "You tell Isaac Mitchell we ain't faulting him none for what happened."

They started to walk away, but I thought of something else. "Wait," I said. "Do you know where I can find Lester Cotton?"

Daisy shook her head. "He quit this morning. Said it was time for him to be headed on down the road." They moved on, and I just stood there, looking at their backs and feeling miserable.

Cinda was setting on a bench in front of the sheriff's office. I went over to set beside her. When Mrs. Mitchell came out, she told us that Sheriff Leonard had stayed real nice. "Too nice," she said. "Claims he will bring Isaac home himself tomorrow if there's no trouble between now and then. Says he just wants to wait until the little girl is buried."

I bit at my lip. Lida Rose buried. It just didn't seem possible. Surely she was over at the café playing paper dolls.

"Maybe the sheriff is telling the truth," said Cinda, like she was trying to believe it. "It is his job to protect folks."

Mrs. Mitchell shook her head. "Not colored folks," Mrs. Mitchell said. "He doesn't like us." She looked at me then. "Noble, do you know where I can find Lester?"

"He quit his job today, told Daisy it was time for him to travel on. He left a letter for Isaac." I took the envelope out of my pocket and held it out to her, but she didn't want it.

"You keep it," she said. "You can give it to Isaac later." She looked down and sighed. "I don't want to touch it. I should have known that man would be gone. It was a miracle that he was here to help once. Twice would be way too much."

Mrs. Mitchell went on home then. Me and Cinda stayed on the bench for a while. I just wanted to be as close to Isaac as I could. We didn't say much, but it felt good to have Cinda there beside me.

After a while her pa drove up in his truck, and she had to go. Before she did, she squeezed my hand real hard. Finally there wasn't nothing else to do but go back to the sheriff's house. I wanted to be there when he come home, so I could watch him. Walking across the grass to the back door, I took to thinking about Mrs. Leonard. I knew she was plumb crazy about Lida Rose. I wondered if the woman could live through hearing about her death. Mrs. Leonard was sickly and so tiny. I wished she didn't have to know, but I knew she did.

Ma met me in the kitchen. Her face was red from crying. "Son," she said, and she put her arms around me. She hadn't done that in a long time.

I stepped back away from her. "Does Mrs. Leonard know?" I looked up the stairs.

Ma nodded her head. "Broke her heart."

"You reckon she'll live?"

Ma reached out to touch my face. "I thought you'd know. She died instantly, soon as the car hit her. Doc said she didn't feel no pain."

I shook my head. "I didn't mean Lida Rose. I meant Mrs. Leonard. You reckon this will kill her?"

Ma sort of smiled then, and she pulled herself up straight. "Mavis's heart is broken, but son, that woman's no weak little thing. She's strong, strong as any person I've ever knowed."

When I helped carry up the supper things, Mrs. Leonard took my hand. "Oh, Nobe," she said, "you saw it. I'm so sorry you had to be there." She closed her eyes for a second. "So much sorrow in this old world." Her voice sounded like she could feel all the sorrow there was to feel, but when she went on, the sadness wasn't there. "There are good things too. That's what we have to remember. We were lucky to have that precious little girl for the time we did." Then she reached up to touch my face. "We are lucky to have you too, real lucky."

Mrs. Leonard couldn't see her husband's face like I could. He didn't look like he felt one little bit lucky to have me. He looked like he'd like to think of some way to put me in jail with Isaac, and he looked nervous, stayed near the window while he ate and kept peering out.

"What's wrong, Dudley?" his wife asked.

"Reckon I'm just worried about that colored boy. Sure don't want no race trouble in this town," he said.

Of course I didn't point it out, but I thought it was kind of odd that if he was worried about Isaac, he was looking out the wrong window. He couldn't see the jail from the south window. Right after supper, what he was waiting for happened. Two strange men came to the door. I was on the way out, so I almost ran right into them.

"Need to see Sheriff Leonard," one said. I turned around to call him, but he was right there behind me.

"Come on in, fellows," he said. "I been looking for you to come."

"Is that your boy?" one of the men asked as they went inside.

"No," the sheriff said. "He belongs to the housekeeper, pesky kid. I'm glad he's going out while we talk."

I had stopped just outside the door, so I heard what he said. I smiled, glad to be considered pesky by Sheriff Leonard and determined, now, to know what the men had come to discuss.

I ran around by the parlor windows and hid in the big rose of Sharon bushes. Right off I could hear the sheriff's booming voice, real clear.

"No," he said. "It's got to be tonight if you want him. I can't keep the boy in jail much longer. Some folks already complaining. His mother's real uppity, got friends among some of the weak-minded whites around town."

I couldn't hear every word of the response, something about a good opportunity and encouraging the coloreds to clear out. I also caught the word "clan," and it made me start to shake.

The sheriff went to talking about a barn on a deserted place just three miles north of town. "Plenty of room for the boys to park their cars behind the barn, won't be visible from the road. You can leave him strung up there. Won't be nobody looking for him there."

My heart raced. Isaac! They were planning to lynch Isaac in the barn on our old place. I wanted to move, to start to do something, but I had to think.

First they had to get Isaac out of jail. Who could I get to stand against them? I counted on my fingers—Preacher Jackson, Sim Harrison, maybe Elmer Keller from the blacksmith shop. Three. There were only three men in town I could count on for sure. That wouldn't be enough. There were colored families in the country, but I didn't have time to get to them.

Okay, I said to myself. Suppose they take Isaac out to the old place. My hiding spot! It was up in the hayloft, and I had found it years ago when I was just little. A board lifted up. The loft had a double floor, and there was just room between them for me to hide. If I took up another board, there would be a place for Isaac too.

I had to think. Then it come to me about the tar paper. Pa had some tar paper in the barn from back when he was thinking about fixing the roof. He never did get around to doing the work, but the paper was still there when we left. What if I made up some balls of that paper, three or four? What if I lit them with a match and threw them down behind the group of men? Tar paper makes a lot of smoke, but if I put wet rags inside, there wouldn't be much fire.

Would the smoke make the men run outside? Could I get Isaac loose and into the hiding spot before they come back inside? What would I do if the men didn't run? What would happen if there was enough fire to spread? I wouldn't be able to hide Isaac, and we might both burn—that old barn would sure go up in flames real quick.

There were a lot of what-ifs. I hunkered down in the bush, trying to think. I broke me off a piece of stem and sort of chewed at it. It would be dark before long. I heard the sheriff saying good-bye to his visitors. I didn't have much more time to plan.

I started to think about airplanes. Basil Bailey was surely at Widow Carter's by now. I wondered how he viewed colored people. Basil sure seemed nice enough, but I knew that didn't really mean much.

The thing was, I had to move quick. I crawled out of the rose of Sharon bush and started to run. I'd go to Preacher Jackson. Maybe I'd tell him what was happening. No, I'd just say I had to borrow his truck. I'd say it was an emergency, but I wouldn't say what. The preacher might talk to the wrong person, who might tell the sheriff.

I run all the way, not stopping till I was in front of the Jackson house. The preacher's truck was not there. Maybe his wife could tell me where he was. I run up the steps, ready to knock on the door. I took a breath, and I noticed it was awful quiet in the house. The preacher's big family was plainly not inside. I knocked anyway, but no one come to the door.

From the lot behind the house, I heard the preacher's cow bawling. Maybe someone was back there milking that cranky cow, the one I heard about in his airplane prayer. I was down the steps and ready to go to the back of the house when it come to me what day it was. Wednesday! The preacher would be at Wednesday-night prayer meeting.

It was three blocks to the Last Chance Baptist Church. I couldn't run all the way, but I did run most of it, stopping once to catch my breath. Sure enough, there was several automobiles and wagons in front of the church. I stood there just a minute, trying to think what to do. Just then the people inside started to sing—"Some sweet day, when the morning comes, I'll fly away."

Fly away, I said to myself. That's what's got to happen. I couldn't take time to go inside to ask permission. Besides, someone inside might tell the sheriff they had seen me. No, I would have to take the preacher's truck, but I sure didn't want him to report it as stolen to the sheriff.

There was a tablet on the truck seat, and a pencil was sticking in it. I could see that the preacher had been making notes for a sermon. I folded the pages back to a clean one and wrote, "I borrowed your truck. It is a pure emergency. I'll bring it back. Nobe Chase." I spotted a rock, so after I backed the truck out, I put the tablet where the truck was parked. I put the rock on the tablet, jumped back into the truck, and took off. I was singing "I'll Fly Away."

It was a real pretty evening, but I couldn't enjoy nothing I saw out my window. My stomach went to knotting up, and I felt like every part of my insides was fixing to shake. It got so I had to quit singing and just hold tight to the steering wheel.

It seemed to take an awful long time to get to Widow Carter's place. The good thing was that it was just a mile from her farm to our house. I could leave the preacher's truck there and go on to the barn on foot. It was just getting dark, but I was pretty sure the sheriff's friends wouldn't go to the jail for Isaac until late. They wouldn't want anyone from church or anyplace else to see them.

Finally I saw the widow's big barn, and an airplane was setting right there in front of it. I could see the house too, and there was people setting on the porch. It was too dark to see who the people was, but I could count them. Four. Surely they was Widow Carter, Olly, Willie, and Basil Bailey. I started wondering what I was going to say to them.

I parked the truck, jumped out, and run toward the porch. I quit trying to think what to say and just yelled out, "Please, you got to help me." I started to run up the porch steps, but I stumbled. There I was, sprawled on Widow Carter's steps. "They're fixing to hang Isaac Mitchell," I said, and I was real near to bawling.

After I told my story and asked for help, I could see that Willie wasn't in favor of getting involved. "Well," he said. "I don't know as we ought to do that. It'd use up our fuel, and we couldn't get back for the public flights tomorrow. Besides, it could be dangerous."

"Lots of folks are counting on going up with us tomorrow," Basil said, "and we need the money bad."

Olly had got up while I talked. He went off to stand at the edge of the porch by hisself. I wondered if he was having a clear spell, if he understood what we was talking about, but I found out he did.

"Do it, boys," he said softly. "It's the right thing to do."

I went over to stand beside Olly. "It is!" I said. "Please! It's a man's life, a good man. It ain't like you fellows never done anything dangerous before. You do dangerous stuff everyday."

Basil laughed. "You got that right." He turned to Willie. "We might as well say yes now. We both know we're going to do this thing."

That was all I needed. "Thanks," I yelled. "Thanks a whole bunch." I grabbed Olly and hugged him. He hugged me back.

We talked about my plan just a little more. Then I was off down the porch steps. At the bottom, I stopped, glad I had remembered. "Gosh," I said. "I need matches, a rag, and some string."

Widow Carter went inside to get the rag and string, and Basil Bailey gave me a book of matches he had in his pocket. "I ought not to let you do this," Widow Carter said when he come back with the rag and string. "You could get hurt or killed. It would break your mama's heart. I ought not to let you go."

"Begging your pardon, ma'am," I said, "but I don't reckon you could stop me."

"Leave him be," said Olly, real soft like again. "The colored boy's his friend. Let him go now," he said, and I did. I ran out of that yard and down the road toward the barn where I had hid when I was just a little kid. I was fixing to hide again, but this time I would get more than a beating if I got found.

The moon was bright, and I kept looking up at it as I moved down that road. When I ran up the driveway to our place, I expected to see the ghosts of Pa and little Nobe. I just shook my head. "Don't bother me now," I whispered over and over. "I got no time for either of you now. Just let me be."

Chapter 10

I RECKON the ghosts listened to me, because I just run into that barn without seeing one thing to slow me down. First, I went to the corner where I knowed the tar paper used to be, and sure enough there was a bunch of it. I took out my knife and cut me off four good-size pieces. I laid the string and the tar paper on one of the hayloft ladder rungs. Then I took the rag out to the pump and wet it down.

Back inside, I climbed the ladder with all my stuff. The hayloft was different than it was the last time I was in the barn. The bales of hay was all gone. I figured the fellows from the bank must have taken it along with old Buttercup and the horses. It seemed strange to be in the barn without no critters and no hay.

My hiding place was the same. I lifted the board and slipped down into the hollow spot. It was a pretty tight fit, but I figured there would be room for Isaac. He wasn't so terrible much bigger than me. I used my knife to pry up another board, making a second place for us to hide.

Next, I worked on my tar paper balls. I tore up the old

flannel shirt that Widow Carter gave me. I made little balls from the pieces, wrapped the wet cloth in tar paper, and tied them with string. I was ready now.

I got in my spot and put the balls right beside me. Then I practiced setting up. I didn't throw the balls, just aimed and thought about throwing them. After a while, I just laid in my hiding spot and waited. I kept pressing my hand against my overall pocket so I could feel Cinda's lucky silver dollar.

A long time passed before I heard anything, but finally they came. I heard the automobile engines first, then the men's voices. How many were there? I tried to guess from the noises, but I couldn't get no real notion. I could tell they was parking their motorcars behind the barn just like the sheriff had suggested. When I heard the barn door squeak open, I sucked in my breath, and held it, afraid to breathe.

"Come in, brothers," a man's voice said.

There was lots of talk and movement. I wondered if they pushed Isaac in front of them. I imagined him there, all bound and gagged, but I was afraid to move from my hiding spot until I had to set up to throw my little bombs.

"Brothers, brothers," said that first voice, and everyone else sort of quieted down. He went on. "We've gathered tonight to do the Lord's work."

"Amen," I heard someone shout.

Laying there in that hot hiding place, a cold chill went over my body. The Lord's work! Down there on the floor of our old barn was a bunch of men who claimed that killing Isaac was the Lord's work. I started to feel sick at my stomach, so bad I was afraid I might puke.

"Brothers," the leader said, "let us sing, 'God Bless America.'"

They started to sing, "God Bless America, land that I love." The crazy thing is their voices sounded good, but I couldn't enjoy the song for two reasons. The first reason was because I knew the singers was fixing to murder the best man I knew. The other reason was because I was steeling myself for throwing my little firebombs.

I eased up real slow. The big barn doors was open, and the moonlight gave me a clear view. Luck was good. The group of sheet-covered men was facing toward the doors, their backs to me. In front of the group, but sort of off to the right, stood Isaac, just like I had imagined him, except that I had not thought about the rope. It was there, though, a rope around his neck, and the end of that rope was tied to a barn rafter! Isaac was standing on a big barrel. Someone must have brought that barrel along because it wasn't ever in the barn before.

Isaac stood up there on that barrel with his head down, waiting. All it would take would be a kick, and the barrel would roll. Isaac would die! What would happen if my bombs worked and the barn filled with smoke? Would one of the twelve or so men kick that barrel before he ran out the door? Maybe. But it was a chance I'd have to take. If I didn't take that chance, if I didn't throw my bombs, Isaac would hang for sure.

"Hang by the neck until dead"—it was a phrase that stuck in my mind from something I heard about a man sentenced to die that way. That man was a killer, though. I couldn't let Isaac hang by the neck until dead, not while there was life in my body.

I aimed at spots behind the group, and I threw my four bombs, fast, one after the other. There was little bursts of flame and lots of smoke. I heard the men yelling.

"What the devil?"

"Fire."

"Run."

There was so much smoke that I knew nobody would see me get down. Besides, they was all running for the door. I didn't take time to use the ladder, just jumped without thinking what trouble me and Isaac would be in if I broke my leg.

I landed hard, a real bad jar, but my leg didn't break. I just held my breath and run through the smoke, almost bumping into a couple of guys.

It was easier to breathe up by the doors, but I still didn't know how well Isaac could see. "Isaac," I called, "it's me, Nobe. I got to get you down quick without rolling that barrel." I knew he understood me because he held his hands down to me, and I started to work at undoing the rope that tied him. I was worried that the men would come back in, but just then I heard what I'd been praying for, the sound of an airplane!

I didn't stop to enjoy the sound, just kept working at that rope, while the plane sound got closer and closer. It come right down on top of us like the airplane was setting on the barn. I heard lots of shouting, and somebody fired a gun a couple of times. The airplane sound would raise up a little and then come back down real close. I could tell Basil and Willie were buzzing the barn and the motorcars behind it.

The rope was finally untied from Isaac's hands. It just took a second for him to get the noose off his neck. "Hurry," I said, and I grabbed him by the arm, pulling him with me back toward the loft. At the ladder, I pushed him ahead of me and told him to go up. We was safe in our hiding spots in just seconds.

The airplane sounds just kept coming. Basil and Willie had been a little reluctant, but I figured now they was really getting into scaring off the mob. Over and over we heard motorcar engines firing up. Finally, it was quiet. I figured maybe it was safe to come out, but I wasn't about to take no chance. "Wait and be sure," I kept whispering to myself.

I just laid there, smiling. Isaac was quiet too, and I knew he was waiting for me to tell him what to do. It wasn't long before the airplane sound come back, and this time we could tell it was landing.

"Okay," I shouted. Me and Isaac both come busting out of our hiding places. I wanted to jump again, but I figured we'd better take time for the ladder. We scrambled down and run through the barn. There was still some smoke, and I felt real proud of my little bombs.

The sight of that airplane with its propeller turning might be the most beautiful thing I'll ever see in my lifetime. "Get in," Basil yelled when we got up close to the plane.

Isaac stepped back for me to go first, but I shook my head. "I'm not going," I said. "They'll take you somewhere safe. I'll tell your mama." I reached out and hit his shoulder.

"Thank you," he said, and I could see tears rolling down his cheeks.

He started to climb in, but I thought of something. "Wait," I said, and I pulled the envelope from Lester out of my pocket. "It's from your pa," I told him.

He hit me on the shoulder then. I watched him climb up in the plane. All three of them waved to me. I watched them take off, but I didn't hang around looking until they disappeared. I wasn't that sure that none of the clan members wouldn't come back.

I didn't use the road, just hightailed it off through the fields toward Widow Carter's place. The moonlight was nice, and my heart felt mighty light, like maybe I could just fly without the use of Basil's airplane. I cut through our pasture, where every step was familiar. Last, I went through a big corn field that belonged to the widow. The stalks were green and real tall for early June. "Corn's high," I said, and for some reason I wished I could tell Pa.

Finally, the big house come into my view. It was dark, not a light anywhere, and I was glad. I had been afraid the widow might set up fretting over me, but it looked like her and Olly was sleeping. Before I got in the preacher's truck, I stood for just a minute and looked at that big house. There was lots of room there, and Widow Carter had lots of land. Her and Olly both worked on the land, but I knew she had to hire men too.

I started to wonder if maybe Widow Carter would take me in and let me work for my keep. It was a sure thing that Sheriff Leonard wasn't going to house me anymore. I wondered about Ma. Would she take the sheriff's side and believe he didn't know about the Klan trying to hang Isaac? Well, if she did, I could do without her. The thought come to my mind that I could use my phone keys again, clean out all the money, and get out of town quick if the sheriff tried to hurt me.

Just then I seen a movement in the shadows on the porch. I jumped a little, afraid for a second that it might be a Klan member. It wasn't, though. Widow Carter moved into the moonlight. She waved and called out, "Nobe, thank God you're safe."

I waved back. "Isaac too," I yelled. Then I cranked up the truck, jumped in, and took off. I thought about going over to Mrs. Mitchell's to tell her what had happened, but she didn't know anything about the hanging stuff. She would be thinking Isaac was still in jail. Maybe she was sleeping. I didn't want to wake her up. Besides, I was awful tired.

One thing I wanted to do, though, before I went back to town. I wanted to see Cinda. I drove the truck close to her house, but not up into the driveway, so I wouldn't wake up her folks. I walked up to the house and went to the back, where I knew Cinda's room was.

I was glad there wasn't no screens on the widows here like at Sheriff Leonard's. I could just walk up to the window and say, "Cinda," real soft. I stood there thinking, though. What if I scared her and she screamed? I didn't want her ma and pa to come a-running.

Finally, I knew I had to do it or give up and leave. I moved right up to the window.

"Cinda," I said, "It's me, Nobe."

She didn't scream or nothing, just come right to the window like it was a regular way for folks to call. "Just a minute," she said. "I'll get dressed and climb out."

That's what she done, too. She come climbing out that window in a pink sundress, and there was just enough light to make her look like an angel. "They tried to lynch Isaac," I said even before her feet hit the ground, and it didn't take no time to tell her the whole story.

"Oh, Nobe," she said. "Oh, Nobe, I knew you would think of a way to help Isaac, but I didn't know you'd have to be that brave."

"I was awful scared," I said. "Reckon I still am. Maybe it was your lucky dollar that got me through."

She come to me then and put her arms right around me. I hugged her back. For just a little while we stood there like that beside her mulberry tree. I guess I never did in my whole life have such a good feeling inside as I did right then in that moonlight.

I knew I couldn't just stay, though, and I made myself leave to go back to town where I parked in front of the preacher's house and struck out for the sheriff's. I was glad to see that house dark too, but of course, I knew someone might wait in the dark.

The sheriff did. He was setting on the stairs, and he stood up real quick when I come in. I thought about turning and running out, but before I could move, he had hold of me, pinning my arms against the wall. "So you're back," he said, and his voice was full of hate. "Where you been, boy? You worried your mother real bad."

"I been walking," I said. "I took me a long walk through cow pastures and cornfields." I could feel his hot breath on my face and smell the coffee he'd been drinking. I wanted real bad to spit right into his eyes, but I knew if I did, he'd kill me sure as anything.

The sheriff snarled like a mad dog. "You smell like smoke. You had something to do with them airplane fellows and that colored boy disappearing," he said. "I know that sure as I'm alive." He leaned his ugly face even closer to mine. "I want you out of my house, tonight! You ain't sleeping here another night."

I tried to pull away from him, but he held me tight. "No, I ain't so sure that's enough. I ought to kill you now, rid the world of a smart-aleck kid goes sticking his nose in other folks' business."

"Dudley." The voice come from upstairs. We both looked up to see Mrs. Leonard leaning on the rail around the stair opening. There was a light in her room behind her, and we could see her plain. My ma was there beside her. "Dudley," Mrs. Leonard said again, and her words sounded stronger than her body looked. "If you hurt that boy, if you harm one hair on his head, now or later, I'll divorce you so fast you won't even have time to pack a bag. Vows or no vows, you'll be out of here. Then I'll see that you lose that badge. Women can vote now, you know. You hurt that boy, and you'll be very sorry. That's a promise, Dudley," she said. "It's a flat promise."

The sheriff dropped his hands away from my arms. "Mavis, darlin'," he said, "let me help you back to bed." He went up the stairs fast.

I watched them moving back into her bedroom, then I run up the stairs too. I wasn't going to leave that house without my things, especially my horseshoe and my marbles. Ma come into my room while I was rolling my clothes around the marble jar.

"Where you going, son?" she said real sad like.

I shrugged my shoulders. "Don't know yet."

"Nobe," she said, "this could have been a good place for us. Why couldn't you just behave?" She stepped toward me, but I moved around her toward the door.

"Ma," I said, "that man tried to have Isaac Mitchell lynched tonight. Isaac couldn't help what happened to Lida Rose."

She shook her head. "Dudley says the boy was driving fast and crazy, said he laughed about what happened. That little girl was his niece, his sister's child. Maybe Dudley done wrong, but son, a body can't blame him."

"This body can," I told her. "I was there, Ma, in the car with Isaac. He was driving fine, and Lida Rose run out in front of him. Isaac sure wasn't doing no laughing, either.

What you said makes me want to laugh, though. You think that man cared a whit about that little girl? He just hates all colored people." I went out the door then. I turned back for just a second. "Good-bye, Ma," I said.

"Wait," she begged, but I didn't, just ran down the stairs and out of the house.

That night I slept on the seat of the preacher's old truck, curled up with my head on my bundle of belongings. In the morning I climbed out with the first light, and I went out to the edge of town to the little creek there. I was dirty and smelling from all the sweat and smoke the night before, so I took off my overalls and got in the creek. I ducked down under the water and come up clean and shivering on account of the air is still pretty cool first thing in the morning in early June. I dripped dry, put on my clean clothes, and stashed all my things under a bush.

I put on my best black pants and my best shirt. I hadn't had them on since we buried Pa, but I figured it was time to wear them again. I was fixing to go to the cemetery to watch them put little Lida Rose in the ground. I had me some time to kill, so I just set there on a rock and watched the water moving real slow in that little creek. I wondered where the water was going, and I wondered where I was going.

At first hunger was a starving critter gnawing at my insides. I hadn't had anything to eat since the beans at noon the day before. After a while, though, I quit noticing the hunger pains on account of the aching in my heart. I just did not see how I was going to stand what was about to happen. How could I watch them put that little girl down into the dark ground?

I went out to the cemetery what I knowed was way early,

but I didn't have no watch and didn't want to take no chance of being late. I was standing under a cottonwood tree near the fence when the first automobile arrived. It was Mrs. Mitchell.

I run out to her. "Isaac? Is he still in jail?" she called out before I could even get close.

"No, he's all right," I yelled. When I got close, I told her the whole story.

She was still setting in the car, and she leaned her head down on the steering wheel. "God bless you, child," she said. Then she raised her head and looked me right in the eye. "No," she corrected herself, "you are no child. You are a man." I don't expect to ever feel prouder or better deep down inside than I felt right at that minute, not ever again.

Other folks was coming by that time, some in wagons and some in automobiles. I guess just about every person in Wekiwa, Oklahoma, and the surrounding territory drove down the road to that cemetery that June day. Mrs. Mitchell and me stood under that cottonwood tree and watched them come. "I won't go close," Mrs. Mitchell told me. "I don't want to pain the parents."

I started to tell her that Daisy and Sim wasn't blaming Isaac none, but I didn't say so. I figured it would be better just to wait and see what happened. Other colored folks did come, and stood back away a space from the whites.

When Cinda and her folks come, she came over to stand by me. "Nobe," was all she said, but she reached over and she took hold of my hand. We was standing there, hand in hand, when the preacher come. His wife walked beside him, and the kids was right behind.

The preacher stopped, put out his hand, and squeezed my shoulder. I figured he'd heard somehow why I had borrowed his truck the night before. When the preacher's oldest girl, Mildred, walked by, she slowed way down and looked at me and Cinda. "I thought you said he wasn't your beau," she said.

"I reckon I was wrong," Cinda said. "I'd be tickled pink to say Nobe Chase is sure enough my beau if he'll have me."

My face got hot, and I figured it was red, but I didn't care. I looked right at Cinda, and I felt myself smiling real big. The smile vanished when Daisy and Sim come. They was right behind Roscoe Jones's furniture truck, and I knew Lida Rose was in a box in that truck. The whole place got quiet, watching Daisy and Sim get out and start toward the empty grave where everyone waited.

Some folks looked at them, real sad. Others closed their eyes and bowed their head.

I noticed Mrs. Mitchell was looking, and so I did too. Just when Daisy and Sim got close to us, I heard Mrs. Mitchell whisper sort of loud, "I'm so sorry. Isaac and I are so awful sorry."

Daisy stopped walking then, and she dropped Sim's arm. She moved over to Mrs. Mitchell. "Come with us," she said, and she pulled at Mrs. Mitchell's arm until she moved between Daisy and Sim. They walked that way to the grave, Mrs. Mitchell between them two heartbroke people, and them holding her hands.

Tears started running down my face, and I didn't even try to wipe them away. I just followed after them, with Cinda still holding my hand. I looked around at the people then. I hadn't seen Sheriff Leonard, his wife, and my ma come into the cemetery, but they was there. Mrs. Leonard was in a big wooden chair with wheels on it like crippled folks ride in. I figured they must have drove in the big gate on the other side, and sure enough the black automobile saying "Sheriff" was there.

I looked at the motorcar and at the sheriff, and I waited. I waited for that old familiar feeling of hate to fill me up. That's the man that killed old Rex, I told myself. He's the selfsame man that plotted to get Isaac hung. He ain't got one decent bone in that puffed-up body. I just stood there thinking all the bad thoughts I could about the sheriff, and I waited for the hate to come.

It didn't come, and I was just plumb flabbergasted. What was happening to me? I felt tired and sad, just too tired and sad to have anything left inside me for hating.

The preacher started to speak. "Friends, we're here today to lay a precious child to rest." Just then he got interrupted.

"Preacher," Daisy said, "I got something that's burning to be said." I could feel that crowd holding their breaths, listening. "It's about Isaac Mitchell." She leaned her head in Mrs. Mitchell's direction. "Most of you know this is Isaac's mother, Martha. Well, I want all of you to hear me say that young man did not do one thing to cause the death of our baby. I seen the whole thing, standing in the door to my café. Lida Rose run right out in front of him. There's not a person here, including mighty Sheriff Leonard, who could have done anything different from what Isaac done. I don't want any more talk about punishing him. He's hurting enough. Let's just have peace!" She did start to cry then, but she got out one more word, "Please."

The preacher opened his Bible. "There's nothing better for me to say than what this woman has just said." He did say something though, and he read from the Bible. I wasn't listening on account of I was too busy starting to understand what was happening inside me. I looked back at the sheriff, and sure enough, I knew I was done hating him.

Oh, don't get me wrong. Sheriff Leonard wasn't never going to be a person I liked, and I sure planned to keep my eye on him. But I wasn't going to waste no more time or energy on hating him or trying to get even. Maybe I was just too tuckered out, or maybe it was Daisy and Sim walking with Mrs. Mitchell between them that sort of broke my heart and let the hate seep out. Maybe it was a little of both.

When the preacher used the shovel to get the first dirt, I caught Cinda's eye. She looked at me like she knew what I was thinking. What I was thinking was that I was glad I didn't have to use that shovel to cover over the grave of Lida Rose Harrison, who had made me her pretend brother. I decided right there that if I ever had me a little daughter, I would name her Lida Rose.

Folks started walking away then. Wasn't nobody making much noise, just talking real soft to one another. I saw Widow Carter and Olly. I left Cinda and went over to them. "Mrs. Carter, ma'am," I said. "I been wondering if maybe you might take me on to work on the place." I got sort of nervous then, and I stopped to get a big breath. "I'd be hoping to go back to school in the fall, but I could still work before and after and all this summer."

"I expect you'd be good help," she said.

Her saying that gave me courage to go on. "Well," I said, "the thing is, I'd be needing a place to board too. Sheriff Leonard's throwed me out, not that I could stay there anymore anyways."

"We've got plenty of room." It was Olly speaking up, just like a regular person, and he was smiling.

The widow smiled too. "You'd be good company," she said. "Your mother too. I asked her before, but she told me things was settled with the Leonards."

"Well," I said, "things are sure enough unsettled now. At least, as far as I'm concerned. I'm thinking Ma might be staying where she is."

I thanked Mrs. Carter, and we said our good-byes. I told them I'd be over to their place in the afternoon. When I turned away from them, I was surprised to see Daisy waiting for me.

"Nobe," she said, "I reckon I won't be seeing you for a while. Me and Sim aim to keep the café closed, sell it if we can. We're going to move over toward Oklahoma City, where Sim's people live." She reached out and took my hand, and she pressed something into it. "Your pay," she said.

It was a ten-dollar bill. "This is way too much," I said and held it out to her.

She wouldn't take it back. "We want you to have it," she said. She reached out and hugged me. "I hope we meet again someday, Nobe," she said. Then she pulled back and sort of nodded toward the grave. "We've ordered her a stone from Tulsa," she said. "It will say, 'Bloomed on earth to blossom in heaven.'" She touched my cheek, turned, and walked away.

I stood there thinking about Lida Rose's stone. Then I looked down at the ten dollars in my hand, and I knowed what I would do with that money.

I looked around then for Sheriff Leonard, his wife, and my ma. They was pretty near to his big automobile. I hurried in that direction. When I was close, I called out, "Ma."

She turned to look at me, and then she walked toward me. "Ma," I said again, and then I told her about how I would be living at the Widow Carter's. "She said she'd like to have you too," I said.

"Mrs. Leonard needs me," she said. "Mavis has come to count real heavy on me. I can't leave her now." She didn't look at me, just down at the ground.

"Well," I said, "just thought I'd mention it." I was sure hoping it was the sheriff's wife, not the sheriff, that had come to depend on my mother.

Ma looked over her shoulder. The sheriff had his wife in the motorcar, and he was going around to the driver's side. "I got to go, son," she said, and she did. I didn't watch her go.

Chapter II

SO I SPENT THAT SUMMER working in Widow Carter's fields. It felt real good. I missed Lida Rose, Daisy, and hearing folks talk at the café, but being outside again felt good. We cleared a section that hadn't ever been plowed before, so I was back at picking up rocks, heaving them at the fence line, or toting them if they was too big to throw. It made me smile, thinking that I was glad to be back fighting Oklahoma rocks.

Some days, just about dusk, I'd go out in the big field of alfalfa hay, and I'd just stand there smelling the sweetness of that hay and waiting for the stars to come out. It made me feel good in my soul.

Two real important things happened later that June. The first thing was the letter from Isaac. It come after I'd been at the widow's for a couple of weeks. I was so excited about reading what Isaac had to say that I didn't even notice the first line, the Dear part. I just went to reading the main part.

I wanted to let you know that I am okay. I am in a town called Langston, over by Guthrie. There is a college here just for colored people, and the town is all colored too. They've asked me to teach at the college this fall, and I think I will like that.

I will be coming back to see Mama. No one is going to make me afraid to go home. I will be coming to see you too.

The note from Lester did not contain a blessing. He did not say one word about being proud of me or loving me. He just said that it was time for him to move on down the road and that maybe he would see me again someday. I guess I should be pleased because he certainly never wrote me a good-bye note before. However, I am not pleased, but you know all about that.

I'm still thinking about how I want to speak out for colored people's rights. I won't ever be angry and full of hate like Lester, but I am thinking of using my real name, Cotton, when I start my new job in the fall. I hope it won't hurt my mother too much.

I can never, never thank you enough for what you did for me. I had said my prayers and was prepared to meet my maker. Believe me, though, I was certainly not disappointed when you caused a change of plan. In my heart you are my brother. Know that you have the blessing of your older brother!

I noticed the first line then. He had wrote, "Dear Noble," and that was something he had never once before called me. I put that letter in the drawer of a chest in the room where I slept, and I knew I would keep it always.

The other thing that happened was that my ma showed up at the widow's door with her basket of belongings in her hand. We was eating supper, the widow, Olly, me, and two hired hands. There was a knock, and Widow Carter went to the door. She come back with my ma.

"Look who's here, Nobe," she said.

I got up and went over to take the basket from Ma. I wanted to hug her, but it never was the way in our family, hugging each other. "What happened?" I asked.

"The sheriff tried—" She stopped and looked down at her feet. "I'll go back to visit Mavis when I can, but I can't live in the same house with that man. I should of listened to you, son."

I wondered how Ma had got out to the widow's place. I knowed she didn't walk, because there wasn't a lot of dust on her feet. I didn't ask, though. It seemed like Ma didn't want to talk much.

"Here's your place, Vivian," Widow Carter said, and she put a plate for Ma on the table. The fried potatoes sure did taste good that night!

Basil Bailey and Willie never did make it back to Wekiwa that summer, so me and Cinda didn't go up for any more airplane rides. We did get to go to a picture show over in Tulsa, though. The widow had some shopping to do over there, and she drove me and Cinda to see the show.

I was real excited about seeing a real picture show, but when we got there, I didn't feel so good. What was showing was _Zorro_. Of course, I went to thinking about Lida Rose, and my heart started feeling like someone was squeezing on it real hard.

For a minute I stood there, thinking maybe I wouldn't go in, but I did. The thing was, I had figured out by then that there wasn't no way to avoid that hurting inside. I never knew when something would come along to set it off. I figured I might as well learn to live with it.

I did think about Lida Rose seeing the real Zorro riding around, but I had me a good time too. It was purely nice to set there with Cinda in the dark, holding her hand and getting lost in the story.

The picture show took some of my money, but I had enough left for what I had planned. I bought a bag of cement mix. I borrowed one of the widow's wagons and a couple of horses. I took the cement, some boards, a big bucket of water, and my marbles. I took a couple of other things too, and I drove over to the cemetery.

I went to my pa's grave, built a frame with the boards, mixed the cement, and made him a stone. I took the other two things I had brought out of my pocket, the two keys to the telephone box. I dropped them down into the wet cement on account of I had decided I would never use them again.

Then I took my prize marbles, and I spelled out Pa's name, Melvin Chase. It looked good there in marbles of lots of different colors. I wrote the years of his life too, 1884–1921. For a long time I just stayed there beside his grave.

I wanted to talk to him, but I couldn't find no words for what I wanted to say. I started to think that maybe Pa was in heaven after all. It would sure take God to understand a man like him. I figured if Pa was up there, he'd likely be able to look down and know the words that I wished I could say.

When it was just about dark, I left the cemetery. Our old place wasn't really on the way to Widow Carter's from the cemetery, but I went out of my way. I wanted to see the old place and the ghosts that I knew would be there.

Sure enough, I saw them both out by the barn. I didn't look much at the man. I guess I was thinking I'd already spent a good bit of time with him that day. It was the little fellow I wanted to see. He had the same blond hair, and he had on the same worn-out striped overalls. He had the same terrible lonely look on his face, too. That look plumb broke my heart.

I didn't get down from the wagon, and I didn't drive close. I just set there on that wagon seat, and I called out, "Don't be so sad, little fellow," I said. "It gets better. I promise it does."

Author's Note

Nobe Chase and the other characters in this book are ficti-
tious. There is no Wekiwa, Oklahoma, outside of Tulsa. I
wish I could say that the race riot also grew out of my imagi-
nation. However, the terrible event really occurred.

In 1921, Tulsa was in many ways two cities. African-
Americans lived in Tulsa, but they were not welcome in
stores and businesses owned by whites. A section of Tulsa
called Greenwood was a prosperous African-American business district. It was often referred to as the "Black Wall Street
of America." Greenwood was a thirty-five-square-block area
containing, besides homes, every kind of business. There was
also a public library, a hospital, two schools, and twenty-three
churches.

On May 31, 1921, a young African-American man was
accused of assaulting a white woman who operated the elevator in a downtown building. The young man was arrested. In-
flamed by irresponsible newspaper reporting, a huge crowd of
white men gathered at the courthouse where the young man
was held. They talked of lynching. A much smaller group of

African-American men also gathered to protect the young man.

Angry words led to gunfire, and the race war started. The trouble moved to the Greenwood area, where the burning of the thirty-five-square-block area began. Martial law finally stopped the riot. However, more than 1,000 African-American homes and dozens of their businesses were only ashes. All twenty-three of the churches were destroyed. The number of deaths, most of them of African-American, is estimated to be between 27 and 250. No one knows for sure.

The citizens of Greenwood were strong enough to rebuild their community, and in ten years it was as prosperous as ever. Greenwood thrived until desegregation made it possible for African-Americans to live and do business in a broader area. In town today stands a lovely building known as the Greenwood Educational and Cultural Center.

Growing up in Oklahoma, I had no idea such a terrible thing happened in the city only sixty miles from my home. For a long time knowledge of the event was suppressed, and no one talked about it. Only in the last few years has the event been chronicled in Oklahoma history books. Recently there have been articles in national magazines, and several books have been published on the subject. I wanted to add a book for young people to that list. It is the young who must learn from mistakes made by earlier generations. It is the young who must fight against prejudice and cruelty in the future.